BEAR

Where Are You
Supposed to Be?

KEN WILBUR

authorHOUSE®

AuthorHouse™
1663 Liberty Drive
Bloomington, IN 47403
www.authorhouse.com
Phone: 1 (800) 839-8640

Published by AuthorHouse 10/11/2017

ISBN: 978-1-5462-1114-3 (sc)
ISBN: 978-1-5462-1113-6 (e)

DEDICATION

This novel is a tribute to our canine veterans dedicated to saving lives and protecting our country. My son Rob spent his career in the Army K-9 Corps. During that time he had the privilege of serving with several different partners. The strength of the bond between the handler and dog is the most accurate predictor of real world success. The dog is always one pay grade higher than the handler.

This is Sgt. 1ˢᵗ Class Barabbas, a German Shepard and his handler SSgt. Rob Wilbur

A handler and his dog can break up a bar-room brawl faster than ten MP's. When working crowd control the handler keeps his dog on a short leash. As with human athletes, it is clear that properly conditioned dogs perform better. To keep the dogs sharp, they work on odor detection, patrol and obedience almost daily.

As long as men have been going to war, dogs have gone with them. **In** ancient **times**, **dogs**, often large mastiff breeds, would be strapped with armor or spiked collars and sent into **battle** to attack the enemy. This strategy was used by various civilizations, such as the **Romans** and the Greeks. Dogs were highly useful for moral, they were just nice to have around. The family pet often followed its master to war and stray dogs were common on battle fields around the world. On March thirteenth in 1942 the US Army launched the K-9 Corps. Dogs were now trained to fight alongside their handlers.

SSgt. Wilbur and his dog Bandit, a German Shepard, gave numerous demonstrations of drug detection and attack at High Schools while they were both stationed at Fort Lewis, Washington. Upon his death Bandit was given a full military funeral, flag-draped coffin and twenty-one gun salute.

Rob and his family spent six and a half years in Germany. At Bremerhaven where Rob was kennel master, he had a Belgian Malinois, named Robbie. Intense best describes this high-energy breed that has become a favorite of police and military units. Malinois are shorthaired, fawn-colored dogs with a black mask and they have a great need for regular metal and physical exercise. Rob took leave to come back to the states for his sister's wedding and to show his displeasure Robbie broke off both his canine teeth on the kennel fence of his run. Rob took him and had gold one's put in place. These tended to help Robbie with crowd control.

To all canine veterans, thank you for your service.

In memory of a few of my four legged companions I have enjoyed over the years:

Snowflake, Dot Com, Strike, Sage, Hooter, Elvis, Kita, Chey, my neighbor Sadie and the best pound for pound was little Scooter. Scooter was a little Jack Russell with a big heart that loved to hunt and retrieve. She made some awesome retrieves for Angee. We enjoyed Scooter and Sadie the longest, some of the best were only here a few years. Shooter is buried here at the kennel with a head stone that Angee polished while she was an art student at Wayne State.

****

A special thank you to Rachel Rosenboom for reviewing, proofreading and her encouragement with this novel.

PREFACE

"He is your friend, your partner, your defender, your dog. You are his life, his love, his leader. He will be yours faithful and true, to the last beat of his heart. You owe it to him to be worthy of such devotion." – Unknown

"God will prepare everything for our perfect happiness in heaven and if it takes my dog being there, I believe he'll be there." Billy Graham

"Be comforted, little dog, thou too in the Resurrection shall have a tail of gold." – Martin Luther

"You think those dogs will not be in heaven! I tell you they will be there long before any of us." Robert Louis Stevenson

"The dog is the most faithful of animals and would be much esteemed were it not so common. Our Lord has made his greatest gift the commonest." – Martin Luther

CHAPTER ONE

A half days ride north of Denver Eagle Valley June 15, 1892

The sun hung low in the western sky, an enormous sphere slowly sinking behind the Rocky Mountains on the western horizon. Its rays, bathing the man and his dog as they cast long shadows across the grassy hillside. The dog looked like a small bear so the man's son, Carlos gave him that name.

They had worked their way over a small knoll near the south wall of the box canyon when the hair on the big brown dogs back stood straight up. He was making a soft, low, guttural sound as he gazed up toward the sheer rock wall of the canyon.

"What is it boy? What's got you excited?" Chet focused on the wall, looking for some sign while doing his best to not let on that he suspected something. "What you smell that I can't see?" He moved over behind some brush and rocks to help conceal the fact that he was scanning the rock wall of the canyon.

There was a slight breeze coming off the wall and this helped Bear pick up the scent. It could be an animal or it could be a man. It was something that got Bear's attention and something that he thought could be dangerous. Chet swept the rim looking for anything out of place but he could see nothing.

Bear began to climb a steep, rocky deer trail toward the top. Chet followed keeping as tight to the wall as was possible. He didn't want to expose himself to a gunshot from above.

Bear stopped to sniff the air and then hurried on upward. Bear was soon twelve to fifteen feet ahead of Chet who was climbing as fast as he could but it was impossible for Chet to keep up. As they neared the top the distance between them grew greater. Chet was breathing hard in the mile high Colorado air when he reached the rim of the canyon.

Bear went around a rock out of sight and Chet heard him growl and knew immediately he was conveying a message to someone or something to "back off." Chet knew from the snarling sound that the opponent was near so his next few steps forward could be greeted with an unfavorable welcome.

Chet came around the large rock with his Colt drawn, ready for whatever threat opposed Bear. Just as he rounded the rock he heard the loud roar of a grizzly answering Bear's challenge. Bear was standing between the grizzly and a boy who was crouched in fear for his life.

Chet fired into the air and as he did he stepped up on a rock to make himself look larger. The grizzly for the first time saw the human and heard the loud report of Chet's Colt. He was in search of food and was not looking for an encounter with a growling dog and a human.

Slowly the grizzly turned. Bear held his ground but he was not anxious to have anything to do with this big guy. Chet spoke softly to Bear as he watched the grizzly slowly amble away. Chet was thankful that the grizzly was not so starved that it threw caution to the wind and attacked.

"Good boy Bear, who do we have here?" He holstered his Colt as he walked over to the boy. The boy had been trying to find some berries to eat, he was dirty and his clothes were ragged and worn-out. He had long black hair and dark eyes, he was tanned a deep bronze from the Colorado wind and sun.

Bear went to the boy who held out his hand and then gave Bear a hug but when he looked up at Chet he had the same fear in his eyes as he did when he saw the big grizzly. He looked at Bear and then at Chet as if to say, "If this dog likes you, I guess you can't be too bad."

"What's your name?" Chet asked as soft and gentle as he could. The boy looked up but did not reply to the question. "You have family near?" Again, no response and no sign that he understood the question.

"Let's get you back to the cabin and find you something to eat." Chet held out his hand but the boy would not take it. Bear gave the boy a nudge with his nose, pushing him toward Chet and they started back the way they had come.

The boy followed Bear and Chet brought up the rear as they worked their way down the steep face of the canyon wall. Once they were on the valley floor Bear turned east toward their cabin.

They topped a knoll and the boy saw a cabin, a barn, several out buildings and a couple corrals with several horses and a milk cow. This was all nestled up against the wall of the canyon.

Bear led the way to the cabin, at the door he stood up on his hind legs and grabbed the latchstring in his teeth to open the door. This latchstring of rawhide was left hanging outside the door to permit the raising of the latch from the outside and was drawn inside at night to prevent intrusion.

Bear went in and crawled up on a trunk with a deer hide on it that was his bed. He curled up and made himself comfortable watching the boy who didn't know what to do. He walked over and stood next to Bear.

Photo by KLW

"Let's see what we have for you to eat." Chet fixed a plate of food for the boy. Some venison, beans and a biscuit. Chet put the plate on the table near the boy. The boy did not take a chair, he stood at the table and devoured the biscuit and deer meat. Eating with both hands he was engrossed with the task as he polished off the biscuit and meat. He did not touch the beans.

Chet put a dipper of water from the bucket on the table and the boy gobbled it up, washing down the food. He wiped his mouth with the back of his hand and backed up to be next to Bear all the time keeping his eyes on Chet.

"You still don't trust me, do you?" Chet on the other side of the table took a chair. "Want to tell me your name, I am Chet and the dog's name is Bear." There was no sign of recognition in the boy's eyes. "What do they call you?" There was still no indication that he understood what Chet was saying. "My wife Carmen, our son Carlos and daughter Abby have gone to visit my little sister and her family at Bear Lake." He spoke as soft and gentle as he could, hoping that the boy would hear in the sound of his words that he meant him no harm, but there was still no sign that the boy understood what he was saying.

"I am going to leave you here with Bear, while I go and saddle some horses." Chet got up and went out the cabin door. His thought was to saddle up and ride up to Kemp and Pat's. Pat was their school teacher and was very good with youngsters.

When Chet came back into the Cabin he saw the boy and Bear both asleep on the deer skin. This could work better, he did not know how he was going to get the boy on Carlos's paint so he put her back in the corral. He mounted his horse and rode east. It was about a mile to Kemp and Pat's cabin and the valley school.

He saw Kemp out by his barn working with a young colt he was breaking. Chet explained to Kemp why he was there and what he wanted.

"I am sure Pat will want to go and see what she can do, tell her I am hitching up the buckboard for her." Kemp put the young colt in the box stall and went to get the team.

Chet nodded and rode up to the cabin to explain to Pat the situation and what he would like for her to do. It was only a few minutes later and Pat was following him in her buckboard to his place. He hoped that the boy would still be asleep with Bear. It was obvious that he was worn out and Chet hoped that will a full stomach he would still be resting. Once at his cabin, Chet took care of the horses while Pat went in to see what she could learn about this young lad. Chet did a few chores while he waited, he had never been good at waiting.

"Kindness is contagious. The spirit of harmony trickles down by a thousand secret channels into the inmost recesses of the household life."

Henry Van Dyke

Chapter Two

Chet and Carmen's Cabin
Later that same day

"Chet this is Wyoming, but everyone calls him Wy, he has run away from the government boarding school up on the Colorado border. He was afraid you would force him to go back that is why he didn't talk to you." They were all seated at the table, Bear pressed up against Wy's chair.

"Wy tells me they took him from his home, he does not know where his parents are. He heard at the school that his parents had been taken to Oklahoma. I have heard about these schools, they want to educate the children in the ways of Western Society. Take away their culture and traditions." Pat had been captured by the Cheyenne years ago. She lived as the wife of Big Bear a Cheyenne chief for over a year and bore him a son. Big Bear and many others were killed at the Sandy Creek massacre but Pat and her son Luta survived. Later she married Chet's uncle and became the school teacher for Chet and the other children in the valley.

"So where are you going Wy?" Chet took a sip of his coffee looking at the boy over the rim of his cup.

"I don't know, just away from school. I know Oklahoma far

and I am not sure that is where my parents are." He dropped his eyes and a look of despair showed on his young face.

"Why don't you and Bear go out and play, you can look around but don't open any gates or run off. Can I trust you to do that?" Chet looked into his dark eyes for a clue.

"Yes." He got up and walked to the door with Bear at his heels.

"What do you think we should do?" Chet took a sip of his coffee as he waited to hear Pat's advice.

"Well, the easy thing and maybe what is required by law, would be to take him back to that school. The government wants to change the life style of these people. They now support individual ownership of land rather than the communal tradition of tribal ownership. This changes their legal status from tribal members to individuals." Pat got up to get the coffee pot and refill their cups.

"Carmen will be home this evening and once Carlos meets Wy they are both going to fight sending him back to that school and I am not sure I want to force him to go back."

"I know, I feel the same way. We could check with Kemp's brother James in Denver about the legal aspects of all this, as a Federal Agent he may know something." Pat and Kemp had battled the government when it wanted to send their son Luta to a reservation.

"He speaks good English, and understands even more. I wonder how he would feel about going to your school with Carlos? He seems more relaxed after talking with you, don't think he trusted me." Chet could be very imposing, he was tall and something in his manner suggested a cobra ready to strike or a wolf about to spring. His piecing blue gray eyes seemed to go right through people and to this young boy he inflicted fear.

"I think Bear is the best medicine for him right now. I think he thought of you as being better than the grizzly but still someone to be aware of." Pat had to smile at the look that came on Chet's face.

"To be trusted is a greater compliment than to be loved."

George MacDonald

Chapter Three

Federal Office Denver, Colo.
June 21, 1892

"Many of the Indian agents hire bounty hunters to track these run-aways." James and Denise were federal treasury agents, Chet was their nephew. Chet and Carmen were in their office to find out how they could best help Wy. Their son Carlos, his little sister, Abby and Wy were waiting in the outer office.

"As treasury agents we do not handle this type of thing but we work with the people that do." Denise was uncomfortable as she was eight months pregnant with their second child. She struggled to get to her feet and Carmen reached to help her. "You will be staying with us tonight, let us do some research and we can better advise you when we talk this evening."

Denise and James spent the reminded of the day getting information on Indian affairs and if there was a solution to this problem. Denise was very active in the political movement in Denver, in the fight for women to have the right to vote.* She knew some powerful people but none of them had an answer to this problem. It was a complicated issue as most all of them had some direct experience with an Indian raid but had little knowledge of the massacres by the US Calvary and the broken promises of the government.

This was the first time Wy had ever been in a city, everything was strange and threatening to him. He did not trust the white man. He had heard about the trail of broken treaties between the white man and his people from his father. At the school they had told them about the bounty hunters that would track them down and bring them back if they were to run away.

*In 1893 the women of Colorado were given the right to vote.

Wy was anxious and restless. Carlos noticed his worried look and did his best to reassure Wy that everything would be okay.

"Mom and dad won't let them take you back to that school. They are talking to Uncle James and Aunt Denise about how to help you."

That evening the adults talked some more about their options. James had talked with several people without letting them know the situation. "If you go to the courts to try to adopt him, the first thing the court will do is take him away and put him back in that school. I learned today that the Indian Appropriation Act of 1851 authorized the creation of Indian areas in Oklahoma. The government has promised to support these relocated tribes will food and other supplies but their commitment often goes unfulfilled as there is so much fraud in the system."*

"Wy is beginning to relax a little. Coming here today was difficult for him as I think he feared we were going to turn him over to the law." They were all enjoying a glass a wine except for Denise, she had apple juice.

"I think our only real good option is to do nothing, say nothing. I don't see where a piece of paper is going to make that much difference." Chet knew what they were doing was against the law but he did not feel like a criminal.

"We can't advise you that has to be a decision for your family and Wy to make. James and I have seen justice work in strange ways." In Chicago, where they both worked as treasury agents they had seen Chicago justice. It was not always legal but it did tend to be just.

*Red Cloud said: "They made us many promises, more than I can remember but they never kept but one; they promised to take our land and they took it."

Wy did his best to hear what the adults in the next room were saying, Carlos and Abby were teaching him a card game but his mind was elsewhere. The teachers at the school had done their best to make them believe the treaties had stopped wars and that the government system would help them. Wy felt the white man used treaties as a means to take their tribal lands and to break up families.

Wy liked these white people but they confused him. Chet seemed to be strong and brave but he did woman's work and Carmen, Denise and Pat seemed to have equal say in family matters. His father was the hunter and the protector, he handed down teachings from his father to Wy and his mother did all the other things for the family. As an eagle prepares it's young to leave the nest with all the skills and knowledge it needs in life, his father did the same for him. The life of the white man was far different and he was not prepared for it. His heart was bitter toward the white man and it was confusing when this family treated him so kindly.

The tipi was the dwelling place of his people, for like the buffalo they hunted, they were constantly on the move. Their dwellings, therefore, had to be readily transportable. The tipi consisted of several poles bound together near the top. The poles were stood up and slanted outward from the center to form the outline of a cone. Buffalo hides, usually eight to twelve skins were draped over the framework. The covering was joined near the top with large wooden pins. An opening was left at the very top as a smoke hole. Because of the strong, prevailing winds sweeping across the prairie from the west, a tipi was always set up with the entrance facing east.

The tipi of his people was far different from the log cabins and buildings of the white man. Everything was different. Wy was finding it harder and harder to hate the white man but he still did not fully trust them. Wy hoped that he could count on Chet and Carmen as much as he could count on Bear. Bear was always ready to defend him should the need arise.

This trip to Denver had him mixed up. So many people, so many buildings and the police in their blue uniforms made him think of the long knives and the stories he had heard as a small boy. The stories of attacks on Indian villages. How women and children were slaughtered while the men were out of camp. He felt very sure, deep in his heart that Carmen and Chet were good people. In fact all of the people in Eagle Valley he felt he could trust. He felt safe in the valley but Denver was a different story.

"If I knew you and you knew me, if both of us could clearly see, and with an inner sight divine the meaning of your heart and mine, I'm sure that we would differ less, and clasp our hands in friendliness; our thoughts would pleasantly agree if I knew you and you knew me."

Nixon Waterman

CHAPTER FOUR

Eagle Valley School
September 10, 1892

Wade and Kemp were walking past the school when the rider came into view from the east. Even at this great distance it was easy to see that he spent much of his life in the saddle. His horse was a large dun, with black mane and tail. As he drew nearer it was apparent to both Wade and Kemp that he was an officer of the law. The law was a bit sparse in this part of Colorado but when it showed up it was not difficult to spot. Lots of town marshals and county sheriffs supplemented their meager incomes with bounties. Of course, they had to follow the rules of due process while a bounty hunter had no such restrictions. Then again, if there's no one around for a couple hours ride, who's to know? This is part of how the West was tamed. Many lawmen straddled the fence between law-enforcing and law-breaking.

Bear who had been laying in the shade of the tree by the school house door got to his feet and moved toward the hitch rail. The hair on his back was standing up and a low, deep growl came from deep inside as he watched this stranger approach the hitch rail.

"Howdy, what can we do for you?" Wade moved toward the hitch rail standing behind Bear.

"For starters, you can call your dad-gum dog off." He had

steely green eyes and a cleverness about his manner. He was not a big man but looked hard, determined and he carried an 1892 44/40 center fire Winchester carbine. He and Wade were both doing their best to read the other.

"Dog belongs to couple boys in school, reckon he could be ornery but he won't be unless you harm his boys. You can step down without any fear of the dog." Wade was enjoying this little standoff.

"Speaking of a boy, I am looking for one. Injun boy that ran off from the boarding school up on the border." Just then the school bell rang and Bear turned and ran to the hitch rail behind the school. He stood on his hind legs and untied the ropes of Wy's and Carlos's horses. With the ropes in his teeth Bear led the horses to the front of the school.

The boys came out and took the bridles off their saddle horns and put them on while keeping an eye on this stranger. They tightened the saddle girths, put the halters in their saddle bags and swung up into their saddles.

"Only boys here are the ones that you see and they belong here, you seen any different Kemp?" Wade turned to his brother-in-law.

"No, nary a one that don't belong here." By now the boys were in the saddle, Carlos reached down to swing his little sister Abby up to ride behind him. Carmen had trimmed Wy's long black hair so that it was just like Carlos.

"You boys say howdy to your Pa and Ma, Carlos don't you be riding hell-bent with Abby behind ya."

"Yes sir." Carlos gave his grandfather a snappy salute.

Wade turned back to the lawman, "You want to light and set a while. Wife will put the coffee pot on, think she has a couple of those bear paw donuts if the grand kids didn't eat them all." Wade nodded toward his cabin.

Bear turned to follow the boys as they got the heck out of

there. A stranger coming to the valley was always a concern and with Wy here, their first thought was a bounty hunter and they didn't want to have to answer any of his questions.

"Those boys' twins?" He was deep in thought watching the boys disappear around the corner of the school house.

"I can see you are a man that can see the whole picture, the whole kit and caboodle, most would miss that fact." Wade held out his hand, palm up toward the cabin. The law man looked at Wade and then toward the cabin as if he was deep in thought.

"I best make hay while the sun shines, somebody in Bear Lake could have laid eyes on that Injun boy." He rode over to the stock tank to let his dun have a drink. He took out the makings to roll a cigarette and looked off to the south, the boys were almost out of sight. He struck a match on his saddle horn and put flame to his smoke. He took a deep drag, nodded to the two men and turned his horse to leave.

Wade and Kemp watched as the lawman rode east out of the valley toward Bear Lake. "Sure do hate to pull the long bow like that, but down deep I think it was the right thing to do." Wade turned to Kemp as if asking his opinion.

"We really didn't tell any falsehoods, he does belong here. We may have put a little whitewash on the truth but it was for a good reason." Kemp went to the school to tell his wife Pat about the bounty hunter. Wade was on his way to tell Judith as he was sure she was watching it all from the kitchen window and would have a hundred questions. No one could ride into the valley without everyone taking note of it.

"A good heart is better than all the heads in the world."

Edward Bulwer-Lytton

CHAPTER FIVE

Chet and Carmen's cabin
October 3, 1892

"I have heard about enough from that loft for tonight, don't make me come up there." Chet looked at his wife and shook his head. Carmen was at the kitchen table looking at some papers she had laid out before her.

"You got the best route for our trip to Texas figured out?" He took a chair beside her and put his arm around her shoulders.

"I think it would be best for us to take the Union Pacific to Salina, Kansas and the Missouri Kansas Texas railway down to Boyd, Texas where Jake and Linda could meet us. It is a half day's ride from Boyd to their ranch."

"Seems like just yesterday we came out here on the Union Pacific but it was fifteen years ago. Do you miss Texas?" Carmen never complained so it was difficult to know. Her life in Colorado was very different from her life in Texas. She found herself isolated in a larger landscape. She got into childbearing and child rearing quickly. She enjoyed both and took them seriously.

"Some, I wonder what happened to our old ranch. It wasn't much but it was home to me and Pa and it's where Ma is buried." Speaking of buried, they were both remembering the grave on a knoll in north Texas where Carmen's father was buried when he died on their cattle drive.

"We will have to go check out the Rocking Chair Ranch. What about Bear, think he can stay here and dad can look in on him?" Chet glanced over at Bear sleeping on his deer skin.

"It's a family trip. Bear is part of the family." She stacked up the papers as if to say that was the end of that discussion. She picked up the lamp and Chet followed her to their bedroom.

Later that night Chet woke up to hear Bear growling from Abby's room. He jumped out of bed to go investigate the thrashing noise he heard. The light from the full moon lit up her room. Chet could see Bear with what appeared to be a snake in his mouth. Carmen came in holding a lamp and almost dropped it when she saw Bear with the snake. It was a prairie rattlesnake a little over four feet in length and venomous.

Carmen set the lamp on the bed table and went to Abby who was waking up and did not know what was going on. "It's okay honey, daddy and I are here and Bear was here to protect you." She held Abby in her arms.

Chet took the dead snake out of Bear's mouth and took it out of the cabin. Bear was pawing his head with both his front paws when Chet came back inside. At closer examination, Chet could see Bear had a snakebite above his eye. He broke off a hunk of bread and soaked it with milk. He put this on the snakebite. Drops of milk ran off Bear's head to the floor.

Carmen came out of Abby's room to see the mess Chet and Bear were making. She went to the counter and got a dish towel to tie the bread in place. "Hope that draws some of the poison out, I will get my medicine kit."

"We can put some hazel extract on it and thank the Lord that it wasn't on his leg, this will swell and he is going to look ugly but I think he will be okay. If the bite had been on his leg it more than

17

likely would have killed him." Chet picked him up and put him on his deer skin bed. Carmen came to them with her medicine kit. She got the hazel extract and a cotton ball for Chet to use and got busy cleaning up the mess they made.

"How do you suppose the snake got in the cabin?" The thought of a rattler in her daughter's bedroom sent shivers up her spine.

"It is starting to get cold, they are moving, looking for a den for the winter. I don't know but I am guessing it found a hole next to the fireplace. I will check and patch up all the cracks." He took off the bread and milk and wiped Bear's head with the dish towel. He cleaned the wound with the cotton ball soaked in the hazel extract. "Tomorrow we can put some Carbolic Salve on it that will help ease the pain."

The next morning Chet was showing the boys how to clean the snake. "We can make a nice hat band out of the skin maybe two and this meat tastes like chicken."

"Why you do this, why you show us how to do women's work?" Wy asked.

"Have you ever seen a Mexican tornado riding a hurricane?" Chet asked smiling from ear to ear.

"No." Wy answered a little sheepish.

"Well if you want to see one, go ask Carmen that question and she will knock your hat crooked while she scolds you on that poppy-cock malarkey of what is woman's work."

Wy could not understand why Chet treated his wife like she was a fellow warrior. His father had never prepared food or helped his mother with her many chores. This would be a sign of weakness. He would hunt, fish, train horses, defend the village, go on raiding parties for horses and all the other duties were for the women.

Bear had spent most of the day on his bed. His face was all swollen and one eye was swelled shut. The boys took turns putting cold cloths on his snake bite and keeping the salve on it. If they were not right there, Bear would wipe it off with his paws.

Wy took his turn helping Carlos with Bear but he did not understand. This was work that would be done by the women and girls in his Indian village. Carmen had told Carlos that Bear was his dog, which he was to take care of. Carlos nodded his head in agreement as if the order had come from Chet. Wy had come to love this gentle giant of a dog and didn't mind helping but he still did not understand the ways of the white eyes.

> "There are three things most men love but never
> understand: females, girls and women."

> Author unknown

Chapter Six

Union Station, Denver, Colo.
December 18, 1892

The big clock on the tall tower of Central Station in Denver said it was ten-thirty and their train wasn't to leave the station until just before noon, so they had plenty of time. Judith was driving one buck-board and Wade the other. They already had their second-class tickets on the Union Pacific to Salina, Kansas.

"Ya'll have a safe trip and give Jake and Linda our love." Judith and Wade watched as they unloaded their cases and sacks. They had gone as far as Bear Lake the afternoon before and it was a nice sunny winter day so the trip this morning had been rather pleasant.

Several people turned to take a second look at this family with the big brown dog who was not on a leash. It was not common for a dog to be running free in Central Station, especially such a large canine. The family and Bear made their way to the waiting train and boarded without any of the train crew seeing them.

With a lunge the train began to move out of the station. The lowest price ticket, third class, would have them in an open car with wooden bench seats. Their level ticket, second class, was an enclosed passenger car with padded seats. Both a men's and ladies washroom at opposite ends of the car. The first class passengers enjoyed the Pullman sleeping cars. They had leather upholstered seats that folded down into beds. Curtains for privacy and porters to attend the passenger's needs.

The train was just leaving the station when the Conductor started down the aisle punching tickets. The Conductor held the ultimate dignity of the train crew. Conductors had to collect fares when folks boarded the train where there was no ticket agent. They had to handle crooked gamblers, and use finesse when explaining to some passengers why they shouldn't fire their pistols out the window at passing telegraph poles or buffalo. At times, they were even required to deliver babies or doctor the smashed or severed fingers of one of the train's crew. He was the captain of the train. His position required diplomatic skill such as explaining politely to a woman whose ten year old son, who was sprouting whiskers, could not ride for free but had to pay full price. The Conductor was paid three dollars a day and earned every penny of it.

The Conductor wearing his distinguished uniform and hat stopped and looked down at Bear laying at the feet of the boys. He raised an eyebrow as if to ask a question when he looked at Chet.

"I hope this will explain everything to your satisfaction," Carmen handed the Conductor a sheet of paper. It was letter head stationary from the US Treasury Department and signed by James Schroeder of the Denver office. It had the seal of the US government on it. It stated that the Wilbur family was traveling on what could be vital government business and that the dog was a responsible part of the family. The letter was full of what deemed most credible, worthy of trust and whereas to presidential appointees of detailed data on condition or reviewing and authorized by this act.

Chet was holding out their tickets but the Conductor was not interested in them he was rereading the letter. He would nod his head, crack a smile, stop and look at Carmen and hold the letter up to the light to look at the seal.

He stepped forward and reached his hand down to Bear who was watching his every move. "So are you credible, and worthy of my trust?" Bear stretched forward and licked his hand.

He stepped back and looked down at Carmen who was giving him her best doe eyed look. "May I keep this letter for an hour or so? I will return it so your whole family can travel but I want to show it to a couple people." Chet and Carmen knew he was not fooled by the letter but seemed to be more amused then angry.

"Sure keep it for as long as you like." Chet was still holding out their tickets. The conductor took them, punched the tickets and handed them back to Chet.

"This is why I love this job so much, just when I think I have seen it all, I get a new surprise." The conductor folded the letter and put it in his inside coat pocket. He took one more look down at Bear and smiling went to the next set of seats.

"Kindness is a language the deaf can hear
and the dumb understand."

Seneca

CHAPTER SEVEN

Kansas Pacific Railroad
December 19, 1892

The railroad made travel faster, was less difficult and more economical then the wagon train or stage lines. The coal burning locomotives, even pulling a large number of cars, could get up to speeds of thirty-five to forty miles per hour on the Kansas prairie. It was a gradual downhill run from the mile high altitude in Denver to the flat lands of Kansas.

At an early morning stop in Colby, Kansas, Chet took Bear out for a walk so he could do his chores. It was still dark and the coal dust and smoke hung in the air like an umbrella over the small railroad town. Chet unlike the others had not slept well, he had a difficult time getting comfortable.

The motion of the train and the clicking of the wheels seemed to help the kids and Carmen but Chet heard each and every sound and could not get his long legs into a comfortable position.

Bear finished his business, came and stood beside Chet who was smoking a cigarette and watching them take on coal and water. The train whistle sounded, telling the crew that the coal and water was aboard and that the train was ready to leave the station. Chet and Bear followed the brakeman and another passenger up the steps and inside.

At their seats Chet took a couple of tin cups out of a sack, "I'll go get us some coffee, the kids will sleep for a while yet." Carmen nodded agreement and pulled her blanket up around her shoulders.

While he waited for his coffee, Chet glanced at the menu. Roast leg of lamb with mint sauce, oven-roasted chicken or pan-fried trout. Freshly baked desserts and fine wines could accompany the dinner. The dining car tables were covered with spotless white linen and accented with a vase of fresh flowers. It was almost empty at this early hour.

Carmen had packed food for the family but a cup of hot coffee would be welcome. Most passengers either packed a lunch or attempted to eat at the busy depot lunchroom, where the service was bad and the food worse. The train would stop for about twenty minutes every hundred miles to replenish the water supply and take on coal.

If it was just Chet and Carmen, they could eat in the dining car but with the children and Bear that was out of the question. The waiter came with Chet's two cups of steaming hot coffee.

"That will be ten cents each, please." He handed Chet the coffee and waited while Chet dug the money out of his pants pocket. Chet gave him a quarter and waved his hand when the waiter handed him his nickel. Everything was expensive on the train and people were expected to tip. Chet felt it was worth it this once to enjoy a fresh cup of coffee.

Back at their seats, Chet handed Carmen her cup of coffee. She took the cup with one hand and extended the other to Chet. He took her hand and bowed his head.

"Gracious God, we humbly pray that you will give us strength, courage and wisdom to make the right decisions for ourselves and our family. We raise our hearts and minds this morning in gratitude and thanksgiving for all that you have given us. Amen." Carmen winked at Chet and took a sip of her coffee.

"Amen." Chet echoed. He was always amazed at the way Carmen prayed. She only asked for strength, courage and wisdom while always giving thanks for everything they had.

Chet didn't pray out loud often, he would say grace before a meal when he was asked but it didn't come as natural for him to pray out loud as it did Carmen. It always posed a question for him. What should he pray for? There were times when he knew he should pray but he didn't always know what to pray for. If someone he loved was sick or near death, should he pray for healing or for the Lord to take them quickly so they did not suffer?

He did thank the Lord daily for allowing him to have Carmen and giving him Carlos, Abby and now Wy. There was always the temptation to pray for selfish things for himself and his family. When he did this he felt shame and guilt not the warmth he felt when he heard Carmen pray. When Carmen prayed Chet felt sustained and strengthened.

"It is a wise and dedicated husband who desires to understand his wife's needs and then sets out to meet them."

Dr. James Dobson

CHAPTER EIGHT

Train Depot Salina, Kansas
December 20, 1892

The Missouri Kansas Texas railway was the mainline between Salina, Kansas and Fort Worth, Texas. It was a cattle train going north and it hauled hay, corn, and machinery going south. It was a freight train with a couple of passenger cars.

Carmen went to the ticket window to purchase their tickets to Boyd, Texas. It would take them two days to cover the more than five hundred miles. They found the passenger car not as comfortable as the one from Denver to Salina. Most of the passengers were cowhands returning to Texas and many of them were hung-over from a hard night of drinking cheap whiskey in the Cowtown.

The railroad had done away with the cattle drives of the post-Civil War era. Now just a couple cowhands would ride the train, get the tally count and check from the cattle buyer and return to Texas on the next train going south. The iron horse had killed off the stagecoach service, the wagon trains and the cattle drives. This trip the Wilbur family was taking would have been impossible just fifteen years ago. The railroad had changed the nation, made it smaller, made travel faster and safer.

Wichita, Kansas had a large stockyard, it was the middle of

the night when the train pulled into Wichita to take on water and coal. It also took on a large number of passengers, cowboys returning to Texas. One of these was Davy Crockett Jones. Davy was a Negro and one of the last to board the train. Most of seats had already been taken.

The Wilbur family had a section of six seats, three on each side facing each other. Bear at times would be in the sixth seat but most of the time it was a place to stack some of their things. Chet was awake, always a light sleeper and he noticed Davy having a difficult time finding a seat.

"I can move these things and you can sit here." It was an aisle seat next to him.

"Youse sure, I don't want to put you out." He stood in the aisle looking around to see if there was another seat he could take.

"Yes, it will be fine. I am Chet Wilbur, from Colorado. My family and I are traveling to Boyd, Texas." Chet extended his hand.

"I am Davy Crockett Jones." He took Chet's hand and noticing the look on Chet's face he added. "My Pa was a fan of the Alamo." He took the seat and got comfortable.

Most of the new passengers pulled their hats down over their eyes and went to sleep. A group of four cow punchers traveling together were awake, drinking cheap whiskey.

"Don't want no trouble out of you boys, you hear?" The conductor punched their tickets and moved on down the aisle. Davy had put his ticket in his hat band and when the conductor got to him, he turned to look back at the cowboys as he took the ticket and punched it.

"Let me know if they get out of hand. We only have the two passenger cars, can't very well be whites-only." He said to Chet as he put the ticket back in the hat band.

It was a time when the States were enacting segregation statutes.

In the eyes of the supreme law of the land, blacks were now equal to whites and must be allowed free access. Whites were forced to share the rails with newly-emancipated black citizens. The southern states were passing Jim Crow Laws formally segregating public facilities. The "white" and "colored" signs were appearing all over the South.

Later Chet got his razor and soap out of a sack and went to the washroom to shave and clean up. He always felt so much better with a fresh shave.

Noticing that he was gone and with the whiskey courage to back them up, the four cowpunchers began to work on Davy. Davy still had his hat down over his eyes but he was well aware of what was being said.

"Must be a Yankee, can't believe he let him sit with his family. What sort of man would do that?" They were passing around a bottle of cheap whiskey.

When one of them got up and came over to knock Davy's hat away he got a surprise and had to back off fast.

Bear lunged to his feet and with his fangs showing, his snarling sent a message to the cowboys. His body posture and gustatory communication let them know his hostile intentions. The quick movement of the big dog had them back on their heels.

This commotion woke Carmen and the children. They did not know that Chet had asked Davy to join them and that he was in the washroom. Carmen looked from Bear to the cowboys and back to Davy, appraising the situation and making an attempt to figure out what was going on. It was easy for her to see that Bear did not have a problem with the black man as he was standing by him in the aisle with lips curled exposing his fangs in a warning to the cow hands.

"I don't know what is going on but unless one of you is good at stitching up dog bites I would back off." Carmen looked around for Chet.

"Your man went to the washroom, he said I could sit here but I don't want to cause a problem." Davy reached down in the aisle to retrieve his hat and started to get up.

"It's okay, I think Bear has the situation under control." The cowboys were back in their seats and none of them was looking the least bit aggressive.

"What's going on Mom?" Carlos sitting next to the window across from his mother got to his feet.

"Bear had a disagreement with those cowboys." Bear's ears and head were leaning slightly forward, he was still intense but had stopped snarling.

"Where's Pa?" Carlos was looking around and his eyes settled on Davy. He didn't say anything but the look on his face asked a question.

"Your father went to the washroom and this is Davy." Abby came to her mother and laid her head on her mother's chest, she was still half asleep.

"Where are we mommy?" Carmen started to answer but noticed that Abby had already drifted back to sleep.

Wy was watching and learning, He learned something new almost daily about this family. There were always dogs around his village but none like Bear. Bear could go from a loving gentle giant to a growling protector in seconds. The dogs in his village tended to be either mean or friendly. Bear seemed to know when danger was near, who was a friend and who could be an enemy. Even now he got up in Chet's seat and watched the men.

Photo by KLW

There were other things that confused Wy. His father had told him how bad the iron horse was but he was finding it comfortable and fast. They had gone from Colorado almost to Oklahoma in just days, they even covered miles while they slept. The white man. They were not all good and they were not all bad. They were different, living with them was so very different from his Indian village but it was not all bad. He wondered where his parents were. Was he near them? Mrs. Schroeder had showed the class Oklahoma on her map. She traced the journey they would be taking, telling them something about the towns they would be going through and how different the land was from their Colorado valley. She had showed them how big Texas was but explained that they would not travel deep into Texas.

"Bear, you keeping my seat warm for me?" Chet returned from the washroom clean shaven and refreshed. He put his razor and soap away as Bear jumped down and curled up near the aisle.

"Bear had a little disagreement with those cowboys." Carmen

nodded toward the group who had their hats over their eyes and were doing their best to at least pretend to be sleeping.

"Do I need to speak to them?" Chet was still standing and out of habit his hand checked the Colt on his right hip.

"I think they will wake up with a bad taste in their mouths and a memory of Bear's fangs in their heads. They saw an opportunity with you gone to have a little fun at Davy's expense. I don't think they will give us any more trouble. Bear saw to that." Carmen said with a chuckle.

"I go shave and miss all the fun and excitement." Chet took his seat and did his best to get comfortable. "I do have faith that you can handle any situation that may arise." Carmen was not big of statue but she was strong and feisty. He felt so fortunate that his trip to Texas fifteen years earlier with Jake and Dusty had produced this Mexican prize. Jake had been the leader of their group as they rode to Texas in search of a good stud, some young Hereford breeding stock and a Hereford bull. Their trip to buy stock turned into several gun fights, a stampede and a cattle drive. Dusty was Jake's half-brother and Chet's best friend. They were both younger than Jake by ten years and it was often a problem for Jake to keep them under control. It also turned into Jake finding the love of his life and moving to Texas. What Colorado lost in Jake moving to Texas it gained in Carmen moving to Colorado.

"Leadership is the power to evoke the
right response in other people."

Humphrey Mynors

Chapter Nine

December 22, 1892
Boyd, Texas

Boyd was not a regular stop for the train so it would stop only long enough for the Wilbur family to get off. The sun had not been up for long and it was still rather chilly but warm when compared to Colorado where they had several inches of snow covering the ground.

Jake and Linda were there with their surrey and Joss had a buckboard. Joss was a cousin to Carmen's father and the foreman of the Bar-S

"Wow, look at you two, all grown up with a family." Jake shook hands with Chet and gave Carmen a hug. He grabbed one of the sacks and swung it up into the buckboard. "You must be Carlos and little Abby but who is this young man?"

"Jake, this is Wyoming but he likes to be called Wy. He has become part of the family. Wy this is Jake and his wife Linda. That is Joss." Chet was putting things in the buckboard as he talked. Jake and Linda were giving hugs and welcoming them to Texas. Carlos and Abby were over-whelmed to say nothing of how Wy felt. The train in a cloud of steam and smoke was leaving the depot.

The two boys jumped up on the spring seat with Joss and the others all got in the surrey, Bear rode in the back of the buckboard.

"Little town of Cotton-dale is just down the road a piece can you wait that long for a good breakfast? We ate last evening in this Tex-Mex café that has excellent food." Jake had the team turned from the hitch rail and started down the road.

"Sure, Carmen packed a bunch of food and we have been eating and sleeping most of the trip. Feels good to get off the train and out in the fresh air, what is Tex-Mex?" Chet was rolling a cigarette.

"It is either Texas style or Mexican style food whichever you are in the mood for. When did you take to smoking, you always said it could get you killed." Jake watched as Chet fashioned his smoke.

"So peaceful in the valley these days and Carmen would rather have me smoke than chew." The women were busy talking and catching up but Carmen heard Chet's remark.

"Rather he did neither Jake but that is his only major vice so guess I am lucky."

"Yes Carmen, you have trained him well. I remember him being a rather wild maverick."

"That's a little like the pot calling the kettle black, I remember our last trip to Texas together, think Linda has tamed you down a bunch too."

"Yes, I am a much better man because of Linda. Not to change the subject but tell me about this young man Wy."

"Well, hope is a scarce commodity for a young boy on a remote Indian Reservation or at a Government Indian School. He ran away and somehow found his way to the valley. Bear and I were out for a walk when we found him about to be a meal for this big grizzly. I hope we are doing the right thing if not the legal thing as he is doing well with the family and at school."

"You and Carmen showing him that you care could be enough to give him the courage to face life without his parents. I remember losing my dad and how much better it was when Wade came and helped us make a new life."

"I worried a little about him jumping the train in Oklahoma as that is where he heard they had taken his parents." Chet ground the butt of his cigarette out on the floor board of the surrey.

"The fact that he didn't could mean he feels comfortable with your family." Jake held the team to a ground covering trot.

"Yes, I think he is comfortable but it is so different and I am sure difficult for him to adjust to. He does not even know for sure that his parents are in Oklahoma. He would not know where to begin to look for them. If I knew where they were I would take him to them. We just couldn't force him to go back to the school that he hated so much."

"Appears you made the right decision. He looks as if he and Carlos could be brothers." Jake turned the team into the roadhouse bar and grill where they would enjoy breakfast.

Carmen was right at home being born and raised in Texas but the children and Chet looked at the menu and wondered what it all was. Beef and bean burrito, served with choice of refried beans or rice. A beef taco, a tortilla stuffed with lettuce, cheese, beef and salsa. Steak Fajitas, Chili Con Carne. There was also steak and eggs and hot cakes.

"Not all the dishes are hot and spicy." Carmen said as a young Mexican girl placed a bowl of tortilla chips, queso and salsa on the table as she waited for their order.

"Did we order these?" Abby asked as she nodded toward the chips.

"No, they bring those to all the customers, they are free." Carmen took a chip and dipped it into the queso.

"What are refried beans?" Carlos asked.

"They are pinto beans that are creamy, earthy and slightly sweet and they tend to be served with all the dishes." Jake took a tortilla chip and dipped it in the salsa.

"What do you suggest I order?" Carlos asked his mother.

"I think you will like most any of it, just don't order it with jalapenos or extra chili powder." Carmen said with a smile.

"It will taste a little different than what you are used to. Even the steak and eggs will come with refried beans or rice but I think it is good to try some new food from time to time." Linda reached for a chip.

The young Mexican girl was serving coffee to the adults, it was steaming hot and very strong. She had to smile to herself as she listened to the table conversation.

After much discussion, they ordered a variety of dishes that they could all share and experience. Wy was surprised how much the food tasted like what he had grown up with. It is were buffalo or deer instead of beef it would be even more like what his mother made. Except for the refried beans, his mother had never made anything like them.

Their first breakfast in Texas was eaten with awes and ayes. The young girl waited on them as if they were the most important customers she had ever served. She treated the children with the same respect as she did the adults.

Each of the children remembered Bear out in the buckboard guarding their things so they saved a little of their breakfast to take to him.

"Because our work is God's work and because He is ultimately responsible for the results, He gives us the freedom to leave it, to trust Him with it and to enjoy the rest of life."

Sherman/Hendricks

Chapter Ten

Bar-S Ranch - Mineral Wells, Texas
December 23, 1892

The Gillette children, John who was about the same age as Carlos and Wy and Susan who was just a few months older then Abby waited on the porch. Between them was their dog. She was yellow and called Honey but she was not so sweet when she saw Bear in the buckboard.

Bear noticed her and did something that made them all take notice. He jumped out of the buckboard before it stopped and ran toward the porch. About ten feet from the porch he stopped and rolled over on his back exposing his tender underside to Honey. It was his way of saying, "I know this is your place." It was an act of submission.

Honey jumped off the porch and went to Bear. She set up and barked at him as if to say, "I am comfortable with you being here."

"Well, looks like we won't have any problem with the dogs." Jake wrapped the reins around the buggy whip and got out to help Linda step down from the surrey.

"Bear tends to live in the moment with affection and food being his main concerns." Chet reached to help Carmen out of the surrey.

"Or the children." Linda nodded toward the three boys unloading the buckboard and the two girls running toward the house. "Looks like they are going to get along fine."

"Don't know about yours but ours have been looking forward to this trip for months." Carmen with her handbag stepped out of the surrey.

"Yes, that is about all they have talked about and the plans they have made. There won't be near enough time to do everything they have planned." Linda and Carmen followed the girls inside, they had a lot of catching up to talk about.

A couple of hands were coming from the bunkhouse to take care of the teams. "Rub them down good boys and give them a little extra grain, they have had a long two days." Joss followed Jake and Chet to the main house. Bear and Honey went in with the men. Honey went to her bed by the fireplace and Bear sat next to Chet.

"I see Honey has a bed in the house, I told Carmen I didn't know but Bear may have to sleep in the barn while we were here." Chet took a glass of sipping whiskey from Linda.

"Dogs are meant to be family. If you can't invite them into the house and love them like family you shouldn't have one." Linda raised her glass, "Here's to our families." They all raised their glasses and took a sip of the whiskey.

"So how are things in Mineral Wells these days you still getting along with the Taylor bunch?" Chet took a sip of his whiskey it was good smooth whiskey but still warm going down.

"Yes, we have a good county sheriff and he has appointed some fine deputies. It has changed greatly in the last twelve years we have more law and order then we did when you were here." Jake remembered the range war they got involved in. "We don't have any men in Mineral Wells like the judge to prey on the weak and defenseless. We still have trouble from time to time but nothing organized like you would remember."

"When an owl comes to a mouse picnic,
he's not there for the sack race."

Old Polish Proverb

CHAPTER ELEVEN

Rocking Chair Ranch
December 24, 1892

Carmen and Chet topped the knoll so they could look down on the Rocking Chair cabin where she had been born and they first met. She couldn't believe her eyes. She had expected it to be run down, she was not prepared for this. It was just as she remembered it, there were even a couple horses in one of the corrals.

"Somebody has moved in and taken over, we best ride in easy." Chet nodded his agreement and by habit he checked his Colt on his right hip.

Riding up to the cabin they noticed the Rocking Chair brand on the two horses in the corral. Carmen pointed to them as she yelled to the cabin.

"Hello….anyone here?" They stopped their horses and waited.

A young hand came out of the barn and another with an apron on appeared on the porch.

"Yes, step down and give your mounts some fresh water we have been expecting you." The hand coming from the barn had red hair and a big smile. "They call me Red, that's Dallas, it is his turn to cook. I guess you are Ms. Carmen and Chet."

Neither Carmen or Chet knew what to say or do, they just

sat on their horses and looked from one man to the other for an answer. What did he mean they were expecting them?

"Dallas has some venison chili simmering and tortillas ready for lunch. We can eat and we will answer any questions you may have." Red walked to the wooden horse trough that was half inside and half outside of the corral.

Chet and Carmen dismounted and led their horses to the water so they could drink. They were both still a little speechless. This was not at all what they were expecting.

"Those horses are wearing the Rocking Chair brand." Carmen nodded toward the two horses in the corral next to them.

"Yes, and there are a few head of cattle wearing your brand up the valley. There is still a small herd of wild horses that roam the valley. We round them up each fall and sell off the culls. Joss deposits that and any money from the sale of cattle in the Mineral Wells bank. He uses it for repairs and feed. Joss wanted the place to be just as you left it, if and when you came back."

When the horses finished drinking, Chet stripped off their gear and turned them loose in the empty corral. Red throw a pitchfork of hay over the rail for them.

The cabin was just as they remembered it. It even smelled much the same way as Dallas was dishing up the chili. Carmen and Chet washed up and took a seat at the table.

Carmen bowed her head and said a silent prayer. The men folded their hands and after a half minute Carmen said, "Amen." The men echoed her sentiment and picked up their spoons.

"So Joss is doing all this?" She looked from Red to Dallas.

"Yes, he comes once a month or so and makes an inspection of the place and there better not be a pole down in one of the corrals or a shingle loose on the roof or we hear about it."

"Joss pay your wages?"

"We ride for the Bar-S, Joss puts a couple of different hands here from time to time. Dallas and I both like it so we have been here going on six months."

"Joss was here a couple weeks ago and said you were coming to visit. He also said that you may sell the place as a couple of ranchers would like to add it to their spread."

Chet was careful, he could still remember the first time he took a big spoonful of chili at this table and couldn't get water fast enough. He took a tortilla and dipped it in his bowl of chili to test how hot it was.

"You don't have to worry, Dallas doesn't make it too hot. Got some chili powder if you want to warm it up some."

"No, this is fine." Chet used his spoon to dip some chili onto his tortilla. It was loaded with venison.

"Sell this place? No, I could never do that. I could give it to Joss but selling it is out of the question. These ranchers do not want the Rocking Chair, they want the water. Even in the real dry years we always had good water that Pa would share."

"That's what we were hoping to hear." Dallas nodded to Red who had a big smile.

"I want to thank you men, my father would be so happy and proud." Carmen wiped a tear from her eye. "If I had any idea it would look like this I would have let the kids come. I didn't want them to see it run down, I wanted them to remember it like I told them. Chet, we must bring them to see this before we go home."

"I was just thinking the same thing." Chet took another tortilla and went to work on his chili.

"There are some changes." Red looked at Dallas before going on. "Your Pa's grave is out back on the knoll right next to your Ma overlooking the place."

"What? How?" Carmen was perplexed.

"Joss sent some men to north Texas to get him and bring him back, it was before my time. Even got the wooden cross that was on his grave, it is weathered so it is difficult to read but Joss got a nice marble headstone with his name and dates on it. He also put one up for your Ma."

Carmen couldn't eat. This was more than she could handle. She had been feeling down, thinking about coming back, she had done her best not to show the doldrums that she felt. Now to see and hear all this, it was more than she could fathom. She pushed back her chair and ran out of the cabin.

Chet got up to follow. "She is your wife and you know better than me but she may just need some time alone. I shouldn't have hit her with it all at once." Red had a sorrowful look on his face.

"You did nothing wrong. She was expecting the place to be rundown. In her wildest dreams she never thought it would be like this. Seeing the horses with their Rocking Chair brand, the fact that her father and mother were both here. She was very close to Carlos and to have his grave here was just more than she could handle. Thank you for your concern and for all that you have done. I will just go and check on her."

"The greatest thing in this world in not so much where
we are but in what direction we are moving."

Oliver Wendell Holmes

Chapter Twelve

Bar-S Ranch-Mineral Wells, Texas
Christmas morning-1892

"I got the greatest Christmas gift yesterday, nothing can ever top that. Thank you Joss for everything. I want you to go to the bank in Mineral Wells with me so I can sign a power of attorney for you to handle the Rocking Chair." Joss had hoped that Carmen would approve of what he had done and what he was doing but he was not prepared for the hug, kisses and tears of joy that Carmen showered him with. Carmen had a cup of coffee as did the other adults. The kids still in pajamas were all waiting for the gifts from under the cedar Christmas tree.

Most of the gifts would be cloths, dresses for the girls made of gingham with round yokes trimmed with braid, ruffles and embroidery. The boys could look for a flannel shirt made from blue flannel with a mixture of just enough cotton to prevent shrinkage. They would all get socks and underwear.

The girls were hoping for a doll with jointed body, flowing curls and steady eyes. Dressed with a stylish dress and hat.

The boys wanted rifles. They were hoping for one that would fire both 22 short or long. They had seen the Marlin repeating rifles but they knew they cost ten dollars and that was more than they could hope for. A box of one hundred 22 cartridges were a quarter for the shorts and thirty cents for the long rim fire.

Linda was passing out the gifts from under the cedar tree. The tree was decorated with red and green garlands and a string of popcorn. On the very top was a paper angel. Linda would take a gift and wait for the person to open it before getting the next gift and it was taking longer than the kids wanted it to. The first gifts to all the kids was clothes.

She gave each of the three boys a small gift, all wrapped the same. They ripped the paper off and found two boxes of 22 cartridges, a box of 22 short and a box of 22 long. They jumped and shouted with joy showing everyone their gifts. Now they had to wait while the girls opened their dolls. The dolls were just what they wanted, exceptionally pretty, stylishly dressed and a little more than twelve inches in length.

Linda made the boys wait a little longer as she gave Jake and Chet each a gift. Chet got a chess board and men. Made of hardwood and finished in black and white. It came with a box of checkers also made of wood in natural and black. This was a game he could teach the children, so as so often happens with parents, his gift was a family gift.

Jake opened a new cribbage board and deck of bicycle playing cards with the American flag stamped on back of each card.

Linda handed Carmen a large gift box. She opened the box to find a royal blue suit consisting of a jacket and skirt. The jacket was lined with black satin with a velvet collar. The skirt was made with graduated flounce, trimmed with satin straps stitched around the bottom. Linda found another box with her name on it and a suit like Carmen's only in black.

The boys were not the least bit interested in any of these gifts, they were waiting for something to go with the two boxes of shells but there was nothing more under the tree. They looked to Chet and Jake for an answer.

"You boys help clean up the paper and wrappings, put your clothes away, get dressed and then bring your shells out on the porch." Jake got up and put his new cribbage board and cards on the shelf by the fireplace.

On the porch Jake handed each of the boys a single shot rifle with a walnut stock, a finely finished case hardened frame and barrel. It would fire either the .22 short or long shells and had a rifled barrel for accurate shooting. Made by Steven's it was called the Favorite.

"These are not toys. They are a tool. A tool to protect you and your family. A tool to put meat on the table. You have all shot guns before and have been told how to care for them. Chet and I will go over all the safety features with you but for the first time in your lives you will have to make decisions about what, when and where to shoot." Jake looked at Chet as if to ask if he had anything to add.

"Bring your shells and rifles and we will have a little target practice and go over the gun safety rules." Chet had to smile at the look on the boys faces and the proud way they each held their precious gift.

The boys heard his words but their eyes and hands were on their rifles. Rubbing them. Touching the wood. The shine in their eyes said how happy they were with their Christmas gifts. Having a rifle of his own was the first step in a boy becoming a man. Wy could not believe these people. They treated him as if he were their son. Giving an Indian boy a rifle and shells was unheard of. The teachers at the school had warned the boys about how they would be treated if they were to run away. His father had told him stories about the white man. Yes, he saw some bad white men on the train and he remembered the bounty hunter coming to school but these were fine people. They trusted him and treated him like they did their own son. He hoped he could prove to be worthy of their kindness and faith in him.

"Do not discharge in haste the arrow which can never return; it is easy to destroy happiness, most difficult to restore it."

Cheyenne proverb

CHAPTER THIRTEEN

Bar-S Ranch-Mineral Wells, Texas later Christmas morning-1892

Bear and Honey watched the three boys head toward the river, they followed at a safe distance. They both could smell the gun powder, the boys had not cleaned their rifles after the safety lesson given by Chet and Jake. They wanted to go hunting. Bear and Honey liked it best going with one boy, two boys were more apt to get in trouble and three boys it was almost guaranteed to happen.

The boys walked in a crouch, their left hand on the forearm and their right hand on the stock just behind the trigger guard, just as they had been taught. The rifle was across their chest with the muzzle pointed at the sky.

They worked their way to the river and then turned south into the wind. They were looking for game, anything that they could shoot. They had their new rifles and they wanted to bring home some game from their first hunting trip.

Several miles upstream, a father called to his son. "I want you to crawl under the porch and get those pups, put them in this gunny sack, tie the sack closed with this string and take them down and throw them in the river."

"But Pa...."

"Don't but Pa me, do I as tell you. We need Lady to tend the sheep, they will be dropping lambs soon. These pups are worthless the father was that mutt and we can't have Lady nursing pups."

"Can't I take them to town, see if I can give them away? They are almost a month old…"

"No, I don't want the town folks seeing you trying to give away these worthless pups, they are going to be nothing but biscuit eaters. You do as I tell you, you hear?"

"Yes sir." The boy crawled under the porch and collected the pups. He put them in the gunny sack and tied the end shut. He walked to the river slowly, head down. The river was running fast from the rains upstream the last couple days. The boy did almost as his father told him. When he got to the river he saw a log floating with the current. He tossed the gunny sack and it draped over the log, he could see the pups wiggling and clamoring to get out of the water and onto the log. It was quickly out of sight.

Bear followed the boys, at one point they spotted a Jackrabbit but it was gone before any of them could draw a bead on it.

"John, what is that?" Carlos asked.

"That is an armadillo."

"Can we shoot it?" Carlos moved closer to get a better look at the funny creature.

"Is it good to eat?" Wy looked to John for an answer.

"Maybe, if you were really, really hungry, we have never eaten any." The armadillo sensing it was in danger, rolled up in a ball.

"It looks like a ball with bony plates on it. Do you think a .22 long would go through that protection?" Carlos had his rifle pointed at the armadillo. Honey barked as if to say, "Don't shoot."

Bear was the first to hear the whining pups in the gunny sack. The log was floating past when he jumped into the river. He swam to the log and grabbed the gunny sack with his teeth. The current was too swift for him to drag the sack with the pups in it to shore. He swam hard fighting the current and angling toward shore.

He slowing made it to land with the sack in his mouth. He was a hundred yards downstream when he got the gunny sack full of pups up on the bank.

The armadillo was forgotten as the boys ran to where Bear was ripping at the sack. He was holding it down with his front paws while he pulled with his strong teeth. The wet sack gave way to his strength and out rolled five little pups. Two others that had not been able to get out of the water and up on the log had drowned for lack of air to breathe.

The boys and Honey got there in time to see Bear pull the two dead pups out of the sack. He and Honey did their best to lick them back to life but they were too late. The five healthy pups were looking to see if Bear or Honey had any life giving milk.

"Wow, would you look at that?" John was the first to speak. They were all talking at once and picking up the little pups. "Somebody wanted to kill these pups." "Bear saved them." "They are so little." "I can't believe Bear did that." "The water is so cold, they are freezing." "Put them inside your coat to warm them up and dry them off. We got to get these pups back to the house. Who would do a thing like that?"

The armadillo and hunting were forgotten, the boys wanted to get the pups back to the house and tell the others of their adventure. They all wanted to shield and protect the little pups and recount how Bear had jumped in the cold, rushing river to save them.

Minutes before these boys were looking for something to shoot, to kill. Now they were looking to save lives.

"Love sought is good, but given unsought is better"….

Shakespeare

CHAPTER FOURTEEN

Bar-S Ranch-Mineral Wells, Texas later back at the ranch

"You need some goat's milk, these pups will die for sure without goat's milk and they don't stand a great chance even with it." Jake looked at the small pups in the loving hands of the children.

"Where can we get some goats milk?" They all wanted to know at once.

"Jose Herrera is the nearest, on the way to Mineral Wells, he has a bunch of goats." Jake looked to the other adults for some help in telling the children that the outlook for the pups was not good.

"You girls watch the pups and keep them warm, us boys will ride and get some goats milk." Before any of the adults could say anything the boys were out the door and on their way to the stable.

"I will give you some goat's milk if you will do something for me." Jose was standing looking up at the three boys that just rode into his yard as if their tails were on fire.

"Sure, anything." Carlos jumped to the ground.

"Take your family some tamales for their Christmas." Tamales, made from corn masa, spread on a corn husk were a part of the traditional Mexican celebration of las posadas, their annual commemoration of Mary and Joseph's search for shelter before Jesus' birth.

"Tamales?" Carlos looked to John for some help.

"Corn husk-wrapped tamales, we love them." John said with a huge smile.

"Some chicken, some pork, some are beef and some have jalapenos," Jose said with a grin. "Good luck with your pups."

"Thank you Jose and Merry Christmas," The boys could not wait to get back to the Bar S with the milk for the pups. When they ran into the house, the girls had the pups in a straw filled box by the fireplace. The pups were are whining for their mother and some of her milk.

"We got to warm up some milk, here are some tamales from Jose." John tossed the tamales to his mother as the boys all ran to the kitchen.

"Tamales! I love them and have not had one since my mother died." Carmen got a look of sorrow in her eyes as she thought of her mother. "Mother made them each Christmas."

"Jose and his family are great neighbors, each year they have a tamale making party the week before Christmas. They make enough for the whole neighborhood to enjoy." Linda handed Carmen the package.

"I can tell which have jalapenos just by the smell," Carmen said with a smile.

They only had one nipple so they had to take turns feeding their pups. They would let each pup have three or four sucks on the nipple and they would pass it on to the next one. After three times around the pups stopped whining and curled up to nap.

Bear slept next to the box of pups, when they began to whine during the night he went to wake Carlos. A sleepy Carlos got John and Wy up to help him feed the pups. None of them had thought about a feeding in the middle of the night. None of them had thought about the mess that five little pups could make either. The mother was not there to clean up after them so it was up to the children. Their parents watched, this was a good learning experience for their children. Despite the good care some of the pups grew weaker instead of stronger. They wanted to do more for the helpless pups but without the magic of their mother's milk there was little more they could do.

John's pup was the first to die. One morning it was off to one side, it had died during the night. One by one the pups died until only the runt of the litter, Abby's little Lucky remained alive. The children buried their pups in the grove by the river. Bear and Honey would sit by the pup's grave each time as the children walked away as if they were saying goodbye.

Some lessons in life are bitter. The children learned this trying to care for their little pups. They love to fill their minds with pleasant thoughts and pleasures. The children had done this with these pups, they had dreams of playing with them and watching them grow into dogs. Sometimes the best-laid plans go awry and our need for answers is immediate. The feeling of helplessness when they saw their little pup lifeless was something they had never thought possible.

The children were learning the huge difference between life giving mother's milk and what they could provide. They had questions. Some they spoke and others they held to themselves. Why? Why was the runt of the litter still living? Could they have done more? Were they somehow responsible?

"You are responsible to do the best you can with
what you've got for as long as you're able."

Charles R. Swindoll

CHAPTER FIFTEEN

Hotel Dining Room, Mineral Wells, Texas December 26, 1992

They were all at the big table in the dining room of the hotel. They had enjoyed an excellent meal when a young man approached their table.

"Which of you is Chet Wilbur?" He spoke with a Spanish accent and was dressed like a young Mexican vaquero.

"Who wants to know?" Chet asked.

"Miquel Brown. I am looking for Chet Wilbur, the man who ambushed my father." The hate and anger in the young man's eyes and voice were unmistakable. He wanted revenge, vengeance for something that happened years ago.

Chet, remembered that night: Chet had Carmen locked in his arms, her feet nearly off the ground. He moved and as he did, his foot stepped in a hole near the bank of the brook, it threw him off balance and they almost fell.

A muzzle flash of a gun, sent a slug of red hot lead at them. The impact of the bullet on the fleshly part of his left arm sent him lurching backward. He pushed Carmen away from him, the quick unexpected shove sent her sprawling awkwardly.

As Chet fell he drew and snapped off two quick shots at the

spot where he had seen the gun flash. The hidden gun fired again, this time the shot went high over their heads. Chet emptied his Colt spraying the shots around the general area of the gun flash.

Lying flat on the ground, Chet could now feel the burning pain in his arm. Carmen started to speak but his hand touched her lips and she was silent. He strained to hear but the sound of his heart pounding and Carmen gasping for breath was all he could hear. Slowly the mental tension subsided and his heart returned to normal. In his mind he could still see the orange-red flash that had been his target. From the position of the last flash, he felt sure at least one of his slugs had found its mark. The question was, how hard was the man hit? Was he waiting for another chance to finish the job? The shot had come from a mesquite thicket, twenty yards or so away. The odor of burned gun powder was strong and the burning in his arm was as if a hot branding iron had been applied.

His fingers found the sticky wound. He worked the fingers of his left hand and moved his arm without pain. The slug had not hit any bone that was a good thing. Funny he could remember his father telling him as a small child. "You always feel worse than you're really hurt or it's a long ways from the heart, you will be fine." He took the kerchief from around his neck and Carmen tied it over the wound on his arm.

Reloading his Colt with just one hand was not an easy chore but it gave him something to do while they waited. They were lying in the open, flat on the ground. It was a waiting game, one Chet did not play well. After what seemed like an hour but in reality was only a few minutes, he stirred enough to toss a small stone toward the bank of the brook. Nothing. Nothing happened. He whispered softly to Carmen.

"Stay quiet." Moving what seemed like an inch at a time, he worked his way toward the mesquite where the hidden shooter cold be lying in wait. Several times he would lie completely still and listen to the night sounds. He could hear Carmen breathing and moving so slightly, the sound of the water in the brook but nothing from the mesquite or his would be assassin. Without exposing himself, he inched his way into the mesquite. The pain of his injury forgotten as his total concentration was on what he was doing. Failure at this game would mean death.

Seconds were like minutes and minutes like hours as he moved nearer and nearer to the spot he felt the man should be, Somehow he must have escaped, there was just no way he could lie so quiet for such a long time.

He holstered his Colt and with his right hand he reached across his body and drew the shotgun pistol. At a short distance he wouldn't even have to aim. He could smell burned powder and something else but he couldn't place the second odor. He reached out with his right hand, still holding the pistol, he felt warm wetness of blood on the side on his little finger. The man was still here, but he was dead. He replaced the shotgun pistol and thumped a match to flame. It was Brown, one of his slugs had caught him in the eye, removing that side of his face. Chet had to turn away as he thought he was going to be sick.

Even now, years later Chet got a funny feeling in the pit of his stomach thinking about it. His mind came back to the here and now. He had to get this young man outside away from his and Jake's family.

"I am Chet Wilbur but I did not ambush your father. Let's go out back of the hotel. Jake would you bring those two empty wine bottles." Chet got up and turned his back on the young man hoping that he would not shoot him in the back. The young Mexican was taken by surprise but followed Chet out the side door of the hotel. Chet knew this was not the time for talk, not the time to tell this young man what really happened that night years ago.

This was a time for action and he did not want anything to take place in the hotel dining room.

"It was a fair fight." Chet felt telling the truth would only make things worse. "I was lucky. Jake would you place those wine bottle on the fence?" Jake put the two wine bottles on wood fence posts about ten yards from where they stood.

"I will make a deal with you. We will both draw and fire at a wine bottle, if you hit yours first I will fight you as you wish. If I should hit mine first you take my word that it was a fair fight." Chet turned to look at Miguel.

The young man did not know what to say or do. He had not expected anything like this. He looked at the wine bottles on top of the fence posts and then at Chet.

"We will stand here, you will say draw and if you shatter your bottle before I do, you pick the fight and if I should win you take my word that it was a fair fight between your father and myself. Agree?"

The young man had spent hours practicing and felt confident that he could beat this gringo. He was quick and accurate. He looked at the wine bottles, he had hit smaller targets at this distance. He nodded his head in agreement and widened his stance as he faced the fence. He would break his wine bottle and then he would kill the man that shot his father from ambush. He flexed the fingers on his right hand and it started down toward his holster as he yelled, "Draw!"

Chet drew and fired, his bottle shattered and the neck and a large part to the bottle flew into the air, he thumbed his Colt and fired again hitting the neck in mid-air. Miguel had not yet fired. He dropped his weapon back into his holster with a shaking hand. He looked at Chet with disbelief in his eyes. He realized for the first time that if this man were a cold blooded killer he would have beat him in a fair fight and he would be dead. He had grown up thinking that his father had been ambushed just living for the time he could challenge this man and kill him. This was not the man that he had pictured. This man walked humbly but confidently. His eyes were not the snake eyes Miguel had pictured but clear gray blue eyes that seemed to speak the truth. This man had grit and had gone out of his way to show him how fast and accurate he was with his six-gun. He had given Miguel an opportunity to get out of this alive and to save face.

"I gave you my word. Senor, it is finished." Miguel spin on his heel and walked away. He was thankful that he was not being carried to the back of the barber shop.

Chet turned to see the faces of Carlos and Abby pressed up against the window of the hotel watching, he could see the concern and fear in their eyes even from this distance. Later that evening Carlos went to his father wanting to know more.

"You never told me about any gun fight, did you really kill his father?"

"It wasn't a gun fight son, and the reason I didn't tell you was that I didn't want it to sound glamorous or magical. It was a different time, there was not as much law and order as there is today. This man was a paid killer and he shot at me and your mother while we were on a moonlight walk. I stepped in a hole just as he shot, the slug hit me here in the flesh part of my arm." Chet showed him the scar he carried to remind him of that night. "I shot at where I thought the gun flash came from and was lucky. Had I not stepped in that hole he would have hit me in the heart and I would be dead."

"Would you really have faced him in a gun fight had he broke his bottle before you did?"

"I felt confident that I could beat him but had he been faster and more accurate I would have had to come up with a different plan. I could see he was worked up and that it was going to take more than just words. I wanted to get him out of the hotel. I am sorry that you and your sister had to witness it."

"Why did he want to kill you?

"We were in Texas to buy some Hereford stock and a stud. We got in the middle of a range war. Sometimes in life you are forced to do what is necessary at the time but what later you are not proud of. This man's father was hired by a very cowardly man to do his dirty work. This young man grew up thinking I shot his father from ambush and he wanted to settle the score."

"Take time to deliberate but when the time for
action has arrived, stop thinking and go in."

Napoleon Bonaparte

CHAPTER SIXTEEN

Bar S Ranch
December 27, 1892

"Do you eat the corn husk?" Carlos looked down at the tamale on his plate wondering how he should eat it.

"Peel back the husk and pick it up and eat the tamale or use your fork but we do not eat the husk." Carmen smiling as she showed Carlos.

"The women of my village made these out of deer or buffalo. The men would take them on hunting or raiding trips. They would eat the meat and feed the corn husks to their horses." Wy began to eat his tamale.

"Ooh, water, I need some water." Abby was waving her hand up and down in front of her wide open mouth.

"You got one with the jalapenos." Carmen said laughing as she handed Abby a glass of water. "Sorry, I will eat that and I will get you one without the peppers."

"You do not make a very good Mexican Abby." John said teasingly. .

"Mom cooks Mexican dishes all the time and I love them but they are never hot like that was."

"That is because I cannot get any jalapeno peppers in Colorado and not all Mexican dishes are spicy."

"I remember the first time I tasted your mom's chili, thought my mouth was on fire." Chet was eating one of the tamales without the jalapenos. His mind took him back to the first time he met Carmen:

"Hombre, turn your horse so I can see his brand." As he spoke, his rifle was trained on Chet's left shirt pocket. Chet turned his mount so that the Eagle brand faced the Mexican man holding the 44/40 rim fire Winchester.

"Step down senor and come. Got venison chili and tortillas with coffee that will float a bullet." He lowered his rifle and made a move toward the cabin. "Give your horse a drink at the tank and put him in the lean-to." There was a small box stall with hay. Stripping off the saddle and bridle, Chet rubbed his horse down quickly with a handful of hay before joining the man.

The cabin was small but it was neat and clean. It looked to be just two rooms and a loft. Chet could smell the chili before he got to the cabin. Texans liked hot spicy food. He would be glad to get back to meat and potato country.

The girl at the stove had her back to him, without turning she said, "Take a seat, it is ready."

"Senor Chet, this is my daughter, senorita Carmen San Juan." Chet couldn't believe his eyes. She was small, just five foot at most and couldn't be an ounce over a hundred pounds. Long black hair and eyes that seemed to have the spice of her Spanish descendants in them. When she smiled, her teeth were white and even. She was young, fifteen or sixteen he would guess and cute as a bug's ear.

As she placed the bowl of chili on the table, her eyes laughed at Chet. Men had been looking at her like that for two or three years. It never failed to amuse her, making her feel both good and bad at the same time. Some men even made her feel dirty.

"Careful, you will drool in your chili" she snapped in a pert, sassy way.

"Yes senor, do be careful. Carmen has the fire of her mother in her heart."

Thinking of the girl and not his food, he took one of the round thin cakes they called tortillas and piled on the spicy hot chili. He took a large bite and almost choked. Tears were coming to his eyes and he had the sensation that his throat was on fire.

"Here senor," she put a cup of water in his hand. "This will help put out the fire in your throat." She was doing her best not to laugh. "As for the other fire," she reached to her waist and produced a double edged knife. The blade was about three inches long and looked to be razor sharp. "I can take care of that problem too, if you wish."

Chet was smiling as he remembered that day years ago. No one at the table seemed to notice as they were talking about their food.

"The deer chili you make is not that hot." Carlos had finished his tamale and was looking for another. "Again, because I do not have the peppers and I also cook so that you and your father can enjoy."

"I do not understand how the cooking and food can be so different in Texas than it is in Colorado." Carlos had another tamale and was going to work on it.

"The people that settle and live there make the difference. In Texas we have the Spanish and Mexican influence and in Colorado you have German, English and to some extent Native American influence." Jake had lived in both places. "Tennessee, where I was born is different from both Texas and Colorado. The people in south Texas on the gulf tend to eat more seafood and many do not even know what buffalo tastes like."

"Yes, the people up north where it gets cold tend to eat more fat and protein and most people in Colorado have never tasted an oyster," Linda added smiling.

"What's an oyster?" Carlos asked.

"It's a shellfish, some people like them raw right out of their shell, some fry them and others like them best in soup." Jake was the only one at the table that had experienced everything from poke salad to enchiladas to oysters to buffalo steak.

"He was a bold man the first to eat a raw oyster."

Jonathan Swift

Chapter Seventeen

December 28, 1892
Bar S Ranch

They were all up early, going to have breakfast and then make the long trip to Boyd to catch the train. No one wanted to speak about the fact that it was time for them to leave so they were making small talk about what the kids would do when grown.

"What do you want to be when you grow up Abby?" Linda asked.

"I don't know, but I want to be good at it." Her answer made Linda smile and wink at Carmen. "I have been thinking about being a doctor but don't think that is even possible." Abby was holding little Lucky on her lap.

"Nothing is impossible, I heard there is a medical college in Pennsylvania for women." Linda got up to get the coffee pot.

"Pennsylvania? That is a long way from home."

"Hey, maybe we could go together, I have dreamed about it but thought everyone would laugh if I said anything." Susan spoke for the first time.

"Well it is not like you have to make a decision this morning, how about you John and what would you like to do?" Chet held out his coffee cup to Linda.

"I want to ranch like dad, raise cattle and horses."

"Me too, I love working with the cattle and horses." Carlos smiled at John, giving him the thumbs up.

"That leaves you Wy, what are your dreams and desires?" Carmen asked, not wanting Wy to feel left out.

"Not to be sent back to that school or to a reservation. I would like to help my people but I do not know how to do that."

"I have heard about a college for Native Americans. Think it is called, Carlisle. I have heard that some of the Chiefs have sent their children to this place. But they learn there what you already know and do. They learn English and the ways of the white man. These Chiefs felt that if they had known how to read and write they could have made better treaties for their people, so they want their children to have this opportunity." Jake took a sip of his coffee.

"Well, times are changing that is for sure, you guys will have more opportunities than we had. Abby, Carlos and Wy, you have a good teacher in Pat. Susan, you and John also have a good school. Right now your job in life is to be the best students you can be so that later you will have the tools to take advantage of what comes along." Chet helped himself to another tortilla filled with scrambled eggs and bacon.

Later that same day in Boyd, Texas.

"Your turn to come visit us." Chet was unloading their things from the buckboard.

"Maybe next summer when it gets to be a hundred in the shade we will jump on the train." Jake looked to Linda for confirmation. She nodded her head in agreement.

"Abby, why don't you leave Lucky with me, we will bring him to you when we come next summer." John reached out a hand toward Abby and Lucky who was curled up in her arm. Bear looked up at Abby and barked as if to say he agreed with John.

"It is going to be very cold when we get to Denver and we

will not be able to get any goats milk," Chet knew this was a very difficult decision for Abby.

"I can't just leave Lucky." Abby was looking down at the little ball of fur.

"It is not about you, it is what is best for Lucky. You know what a Colorado winter can be like." Carmen had been worried about Lucky on the trip and with them coming next summer it could be a way for Lucky not to have to brave the winter. "When you take on the responsibility you have to do what is best for Lucky not what is best for you." She knew Abby would be sad and cry most of the way home but that may be better than to have Lucky suffer and die on the trip.

"Are you telling me to leave Lucky, that I can't take him with me?"

"No, it is your decision, he is your responsibility to care for. Your father and I just want you to know that you do have an option." In the back of her mind Carmen was also thinking this would make sure they came to visit.

"This is not fair." Big tears formed in the corner of her eyes.

"You still have some time, take a walk. The train won't be here for a half hour or so." Chet and Jake had the last of their things out of the wagon and the station master was putting up the white flag to signal the train to stop in Boyd.

Abby felt as if her heart would break. She turned her back on everyone and Bear followed as she walked away. She found a grassy spot around the corner of the depot out of sight and sat down. She could not hold back the tears. Bear pushed up against her as if to give his support. Bear licked her hand holding Lucky. She reached out with her other arm and hugged Bear, sobbing softly. They stayed like that until she heard the train whistle and the rumble of the iron horse coming into the depot. She got up as if in a daze and walked back to the others waiting on the platform. Without saying anything she handed Lucky to John. Bear pressed up against her leg. Susan who was also sobbing gave her a hug. "We will take good care of Lucky for you." Her words were very difficult to understand as she was taking short quick breaths as she sobbed.

Everyone was saying their goodbyes, giving hugs and shaking hands. Tears were flowing from smiling faces. It had been a good visit but the days had gone too quickly. The train came to a stop and the conductor stepped out and yelled, "All aboard!"

None of them were in a haste to get on the train but they knew it would not wait long. Jake and John helped with the baggage and the conductor held up his hand when Bear followed them onto the train. Carmen handed him the letter she had successfully used on their trip to Texas. He was reading the letter as Jake and John stepped off the train and onto the platform.

The conductor was still holding the letter when he took the tickets from Chet. He punched their tickets and handed them and the letter to Chet. "This is very irregular, that animal causes the least bit of trouble and it is off the train."

Bear got up in the seat with Abby who was still sobbing. The conductor wondered what that was all about but did not ask.

The trip back to Denver was uneventful and seemed to go faster than their trip south. The boys were planning all the hunting trips they could take with their new rifles. After a good nap leaning on Bear, Abby woke up in a better mood and she woke up hungry.

"What we got to eat, I am starving." Abby was still leaning on Bear's warm body, that and the motion of the train had helped her take a much needed nap.

"Happy trails to you, until we meet again. Some trails are happy ones, others are blue. It's the way you ride the trail that counts. Here's a happy one for you."

Dale Evans

CHAPTER EIGHTEEN

January 1, 1893
Union Station, Denver

The super moon illuminated the night sky and reflected off the snow. It was near mid-night when the train pulled into Union Station. Wade was waiting with the team and buckboard. The plan had been to go to the Windsor Hotel, spend the night and get an early start the next morning. "Looks like we could have a storm moving in, think we best load up and drive to Bear Lake." Wade was putting their bags in the back of the buckboard. Dusty and Sarah owned the trading post at Bear Lake. Sarah was Wade's daughter and Chet's sister.

"Whatever you think is best Dad, I would rather be at Bear Lake than Denver if a Northerner blows in." Chet was taking the horse blankets and making a comfortable spot for Carmen and the children. He and Wade would ride on the spring seat with a horse blanket over their legs. It was cold but the full moon in the clear sky would provide the light they needed to guide the team.

"Dad thinks we should go to Bear Lake, he thinks a storm could be coming." Chet was helping Carmen into the buckboard.

"That is fine with me, by the time we got to the hotel and asleep it would be time to get up." She put one boy on each side of her and Abby between her legs. Bear was curled up next to

Carlos. They had horse blankets under and over them. Bear Lake was about half way to their cabin in Eagle Valley, a little over two hours on a good day.

The wheels made a crunching sound on the hard packed snow as Wade turned the team away from the hitch rail. The matched pair of blacks were tired of standing and were eager to be on the move. When Wade turned them north off of Denver's main street the team knew they were headed toward their barn and picked up the pace. The beauty of the rolling prairie in the moon light was something special to behold. In the distance they heard a wolf give a long, mournful howl at the moon.

Photo by Rachel Rosenboom

The wind swung to the northwest and it had a colder bite to it as it came off the Rocky Mountains. Chet and Wade pulled down their hats and turned up their collars, they both pulled the kerchiefs around their necks up over their nose. Driving into the cross wind made it feel even colder than it was.

"Going to get some snow, I can feel it in the air." Wade turned to Chet as he spoke.

"Hope we can make Bear Lake before it gets too bad." Chet and Wade both knew now fast a Northerner could develop. Coming off the Rockies the moon could be big and bright one minute and they could experience a whiteout the next. Being caught out in the open in a Colorado blizzard would not be a good thing.

The team was fresh and their load not that heavy so they held a good pace. It was not long before the men could feel a little snow spitting in the wind. Wade spoke to the team and put them into a ground covering trot. Visibility was still good and Mr. Moon was doing his best to show the road to Dusty and Sarah's trading post at Bear Lake.

"This is going to get worse before it gets better, the question is, how long before it becomes a problem?" Chet knew his father was a good judge of the weather.

"Hard to say." Wade looked up at the clouds moving across the face of the moon. "I think we can be enjoying a hot cup of coffee with Dusty and Sarah before our visibility gets too bad." Chet heard what he thought was more hope than conviction in Wade's words. He adjusted the horsehide blanket they had over their laps and put his arms under it. He was on the west side, the wind side of the spring seat which helped to give his father a little protection.

"Let me know when you want me to drive so you can warm up your arms." Wade was wearing heavy horsehide mittens with knitted wool wrist bands so his hands were fine. He was wearing wool winter underwear, a heavy winter weight flannel shirt and his oil tanned horsehide coat but holding the reins the Colorado wind got to his arms.

The team was holding a good steady pace, eating up the miles to Bear Lake. The kids and Bear were sleeping but Carmen could hear the wind, the sound of the horse's hoofs on the frozen ground and the crunch of the wheels and could not drift off to sleep.

Wade was glad that he had used the bridles with the blinders. The leather flap to keep the horse from seeing sideways they also gave the horses' protection from the driving snow.

Photo by Steve Rosenboom

Chet couldn't help but remember how comfortable the train had been, how warm and safe. How fast they had covered the many miles from Texas to Denver. This was much slower, more dangerous as storms were a constant source of concern. He had grown up with the hardships of travel in Colorado but the precious cargo, more valuable than gold, under the horse blankets in the buckboard gave him a troubled state of mind. If it were just him and his father he would not worry.

It was beginning to snow harder, the wind whipped the snow so that it seemed to be almost parallel to the ground. The snow driven by the wind began to drift across the road. It was a dry snow, frozen crystals not soft white flakes floating to the ground. In places where there was a tree or bush near the side of the road drifts were beginning to form.

"How much longer do you think we have before this turns into a real blizzard?" Chet had to turn his head and almost yell for Wade to hear. The wind and the heavy beaver hat Wade was wearing made it difficult for him to hear.

"Can't say. The road will start to bend to the northeast soon which will help. Once we get around the corner of the lake we should be okay." Once around the northwest corner of Bear Lake they would have the wind almost at their backs. It was only four or five miles from there to Dusty and Sarah's outpost and safety.

The super moon that had illuminated the Colorado sky was now hidden by storm clouds and driving snow. It was difficult to see. The horses could see better than Wade so he gave them a loose rein and let them lead the way. The natural thing for a horse to do in a storm like this was to turn its butt to the wind and drift with the wind until it could find shelter.

Both Wade and Chet knew that if either of two things happened they would be in more trouble. If it stopped snowing the temperature would drop and it could get very cold or if the drifts got too deep the horses would not be able to pull the buckboard through the drifts. They had both seen wind-whipped snowdrifts over a man's head. The salt-like snow drifted across the road but was not piling up which was good for these travelers.

They had just rounded the northwest corner of Bear Lake and began to go eastward toward the trading post when the right front wheel of the buckboard hit a large rock hidden by the snow. The wheel, brittle from the cold, broke and dug into the packed snow. Wade pulled up the team.

"We just broke a wheel, we cannot continue with the buckboard." Wade wrapped the reins around the whip holder and slid off the seat onto the ground. The rig was leaning to the right so Chet slide over and followed Wade.

"Let's unhitch the team, Carmen and Abby can ride one horse and the boys the other." Wade began to unhitch the trace tugs of the harness.

"Why have we stopped? Is there a problem?" Carmen asked as she poked her head out from under the horse blanket.

"Yes, we broke a wheel. Wake up the kids, you and Abby will ride one horse the boys the other." Chet took the horse blanket they had been using and folding it in half he put it over the horse's back. He left the harness in place. Wade was doing the same to the other horse. He and Wade would lead the horses, they would have to leave the buckboard and their bags.

The kids had a hundred questions as they sleepily crawled out of the buckboard. Chet and Wade did their best to answer as many as they could and give them assurance that it was going to be okay as they got them on the horses and wrapped the horse blankets over their shoulders. Bear jumped out of the rig and took his position at the head of the column.

The wind was at their backs which helped greatly. The road was snow packed and had large drifts in spots. The whoosh of the wind in the evergreens and tall white birch made them realize how powerful Mother Nature could be and they were thankful that the storm wasn't worse. They knew the worst part of winter was ahead of them. There would be days on end that they would be snowed in. They were not forced to live in Eagle Valley so far from Denver, it was their choice. They felt the good far outweighed the bad.

Bear was glad to be out of the buckboard. He lifted his leg and peed on a tree beside the road. Chet chuckled to himself as he remembered his dad telling him, when he was a small boy, never to eat the yellow snow. Of course he had to pass on this wisdom to his son Carlos.

With Bear out front and Wade leading his horse behind him they started for the outpost. Wade and his horse broke a path for Chet and his horse. Wade had difficulty walking as some of the drifts were high and he had to lift his feet to get through. Bear would stop and turn to look back at the caravan following and after a few hundred yards he veered off the road toward the lake. He followed a game trail at the edge of the lake.

Wade stopped and watched Bear, after thinking about it a moment, he followed. Once on the game trail it was easier going, very few drifts and the trees and bank protected them from the wind and the driving snow. It was much easier walking for Wade and they made better time. There was a time or two, the riders had to duck under a tree limb. Wade and Chet would slow down or stop and let them know about the low overhang, once they even had to dismount as the tree branch was so low Wade had to hold it up for the horses to get under it. Another spot the horses had to leap over a fallen tree but it was still easier and faster than the drifted road.

"We often take for granted the very things
that most deserve our gratitude."

Ozick

CHAPTER NINETEEN

January 2, 1893
Bear Lake Trading Post

"Dad I am sure glad you thought to follow the game trail."

"I can't take credit for that, it was Bear that showed me the way." The men were helping the riders unwrap and dismount. Bear went to the door and barked. After a few minutes, Dusty appeared with a lantern and his shotgun.

"We can use the lantern but you won't need the shotgun." Chet said as he helped Carmen and Abby off the horse. Chet and Dusty grew up neighbors in Eagle Valley. They were the best of friends and very competitive. Everything was a contest with them. Chet was the fastest and best shot with a hand-gun, Dusty was the best with a rifle, Chet was the best at throwing a rope, Dusty at bulldogging, Chet was the fastest of foot, Dusty the biggest and strongest, they loved to badger each other but it got annoying to Carmen and Sarah.

"You're right about that, I can handle you without a gun." Dusty held out his hand to Abby, helping her up on the porch of the Trading Post. "Good to see you young lady, didn't expect you until tomorrow. Get yourself out of the cold and in where it is warm. Your Aunt Sarah will be making coffee and hot cocoa." *

"You boys take the horses to the lean-to and hang the harness on the wall, rub them down and give them some hay and grain and by then the hot coco will be ready." Dusty pointed toward the lean-to at the back of the trading post. "What happened to your rig?"

"Broke a wheel near the west end of the lake." Chet was helping Carmen up on the porch. Wade was picking up the horse blankets.

"Let me give you a hand with that." Dusty said as he took one end of the heavy blanket to help Wade fold it. "I got a spare wheel in the sled, we can take the bobsled in the morning to fetch your rig back here."

*The first chocolate beverage is believed to have been created by the Maya around 2,000 years ago and a cocoa beverage was an essential part of Aztec culture by 1400.

Bobsleds were designed to be used in deep snow. The runners on the bobsled were heavy and wide. The front runners were designed to turn or steer the larger rig through the snow. This made it more functional in deep snow than the sleigh with its one narrow runner.

"I wished half way from Denver that I had my bobsled but when I left the valley there was no snow. I will leave the buckboard here and either I or Chet will ride to the valley and return with my bobsled." They had the blankets all folded and stacked on the porch.

"Let's go get a cup of hot coffee." Dusty opened the door for Wade.

They were all seated around the big kitchen table enjoying a hot cup of coffee or cocoa. Carmen had her little niece on her lap but when she saw her grandfather she scrambled down and ran to Wade. "Well I guess that shows me who the favorite is." Carmen said with a chuckle.

"So tell me all about your trip, how was Texas?" Sarah was getting Dusty and Wade some coffee.

"It was a great trip, no major problems until we broke the wheel." Chet took the coffee from his sister and took a seat.

The back door opened and the boys burst in bringing a draft of cold air with them. "We did as you told us, horses are all taken care of."

"Come get some hot cocoa and a sugar cookie, you have earned it." Sarah handed them the big cookie jar. They told of their trip and how Jake and Linda were planning to come visit during the summer.

"Was Bear a problem?" Sarah nodded toward him laying by the door.

"No, in fact he was very helpful a couple of times." Carmen got up to get more coffee off the cook stove.

"He was very helpful tonight finding that game trail." Wade held out his cup to Carmen to top off. "Don't know why I didn't think of it."

"Bear is the smartest dog, he is always doing things like that. You sure do make good sugar cookies Aunt Sarah." Carlos was talking with his mouth full of the last bite of his cookie.

"Have another", she smiled as she handed the boys the white glazed stoneware cookie jar.

They talked of their trip and of their plans for tomorrow. It was still snowing so they would have to wait and see what it was like when the sun came up. It was late, Wade and Chet were exhausted from walking in the cold and snow. Being in the warmth made them sleepy, so when Wade yawned they all knew it was time to find a nest for the short time they had to sleep. Bear was already curled up sleeping by the door.

> "There is only one smartest dog in the
> world and every boy has it."
>
> Unknown

CHAPTER TWENTY

April 20, 1893
Chet & Carmen's Cabin

Bear's sensitive ears heard what no one else in the cabin could hear. The sound made him jump off his deer skin bed and go to the door. He pulled the latch string of rawhide and opened the door. Pushing it closed behind him he turned to go down the steps and check on the noise. Only a sliver of a Colorado moon was in the clear blue sky but it was enough for Bear to find his way.

Photo by Rachel Rosenboom

Out of the yard and toward the stream he raced, the sound of a fight becoming clearer and clearer. Topping a small knoll he saw a small pack of wolves attacking a doe who was protecting her small fawn. One of the pack lay on the ground a victim of the doe's sharp hoofs. The pack was beginning to win the battle as she was bleeding badly. Bear with a loud growl joined the fight. Coming up behind them he grabbed one of the wolves by the nap of his neck and with a deep bite and shake of his head he threw the smaller wolf to the side. Quickly he moved forward and stood beside the doe, showing his fangs and with a deep low angry sound let the two remaining wolves know he would fight.

These two already had marks from the doe's front feet as she had struck out to fight them. The wolf Bear had attacked was getting up but not showing any great interest in fighting. Slowly the wolves backed away. They could smell blood and did not want to abandon their feast but they also did not want to recklessly attack. The doe was weak from fighting and the loss of blood. It did not appear that any of the fangs of the wolves had found an artery or major vain, had that been the case she would bleed out quickly.

Bear stood guard as the doe went to her fawn and laid down. It was still a couple hours until dawn and Bear knew the wolves were in the darkness waiting for a chance to finish their kill.

A couple hours later, back in the cabin, a sleepy Chet went out on the porch to relieve himself. Bear always followed him out and found a tree but this morning he was not there.

"Carlos, Wy! Boys get up, Bear is not here we have to go find out why." Chet was jumping into his clothes and pulling on his boots on as his mind was trying to figure out why Bear was not there as usual.

They hurried out to the barn and saddled their horses. Mr. Sun was just coming up when they rode out of the yard. "Wy you ride to the south and call for Bear. Carlos you ride to the west and do the same. I will go to the north. If you see or hear Bear ride north to me." They all took off at a trot calling to Bear as they went.

They would stop and listen from time to time to see if they could hear anything.

Bear heard them call and began to bark. It was Chet that heard him first and he fired his colt into the air to signal the boys that he had found Bear. The wolves heard the shot and smelled the human and his horse coming so they turned tail and ran.

Carlos, slid his horse to a stop and jumped off. "What are we going to do Dad? The doe looks like she has been hurt." As Carlos asked the question Wy rode up from the south.

"Yes, the doe is weak, that could help us. You boys go and fetch the buckboard, I will stay here with Bear in case the wolves circle back."

In less than an hour the boys were back with the buckboard. Chet had them back up the buckboard as near the doe as was possible. He dropped the tail gate and told Bear to jump up in the back. Bear leaped into the buckboard and Chet went to the fawn. They were lucky, it was newborn. Had the fawn been even a week old it would have fought them. Chet gathered the fawn up in his arms and laid it in the buckboard next to Bear.

"This is going to be the tough part. You boys help me lift the doe, be careful of her feet they are sharp and she could break your arm, Carlos grab her right front leg, just above the ankle, put your other arm under her chest. Wy you do the same to her left leg. I will grab her hind legs with one hand and put my other arm under her hips. We will do it all at once when I give the command. Any questions?"

The boys had a hundred questions but didn't know which to ask first. Rather than ask a question they just said, "No, Sir," at the same time.

"Okay, ready....go." They all moved as one and grabbed the injured doe. She was too weak to fight very much and allowed them to lift her into the back of the buckboard with her fawn and Bear.

"You boys bring the buckboard, I will ride ahead and get the box stall ready." Without another word, Chet mounted his horse and took off for home.

When the boys pulled into the yard, Carmen and Abby were in the box stall with the home medicine kit. The boys backed the buckboard up at close as they could and jumped out to help Chet. The doe was too weak to fight. They carried her in and placed her in the box stall, Carmen and Abby went to work. They applied hazel extract with cotton balls to stop the bleeding and clean the wounds. They covered the wounds with carbolic salve. While they were doing this Chet and the boys went to the kitchen and made a mash of corn meal and hot water. They took this and a fresh bucket of water with Carmen's turkey baster out to the barn.

Chet would squeeze the bulb on the baster and load it with water to squirt into the side of the doe's mouth. After a couple of these they spooned fed her some mash and washed it down with water. She was too weak and tried to resist them. They also moved the fawn into a position so it could nurse. The doe had plenty of milk and the fawn ate hungrily.

After of week of this TLC the doe was up and eating hay and grain. The fawn pranced around showing no fear of the humans but the doe was still leery of them. She was more relaxed when Bear was there standing between her and these humans.

They turned them out into a small circular corral where the doe had more room to exercise and gain her strength back. In good health the doe could have cleared the pole fence with ease but with the fawn and still not a hundred percent she made no attempt to escape. After another few days Chet told the boys to leave the gate open. The next morning the corral was empty.

A day later the boys noticed that the doe had come back during the night to eat some hay and grain. Each day they would put fresh hay and grain in the corral and each morning it would be gone. The doe was remaining near.

"Think she just feels safer during the day to hide in the brush with her fawn. At night she comes out to graze and finds her way to the corral."

"Dad, I am confused."

"About what Abby?"

"Well, we have spent a great deal of time and effort with this doe and fawn and yet this fall or winter you and Carlos will go deer hunting."

"Abby, our Lord put man on earth to be dominant over all the animals, the fish and fowl. He intends for man to eat them to nourish their bodies so they can do His work. He also gave us compassion. This compassion is what keeps us from hunting during the time of the year they are nursing. We do the same with our animals, we never butcher a cow when she has a calf at her side or a chicken when it has baby chicks. We do not hunt just to kill. We hunt for food and to protect each other and our stock. If a bear comes into the valley to kill our stock we will track it down. The same is true for a man, if someone comes into the valley and does any of us harm, the others will track him down. This is complicated. Your great grandfather can explain it far better than I can. You should ask Jokob any questions you have during our bible study, he would like that."

Chet was proud of his children and the way they took care of this doe and her fawn. This time their work paid off. He knew it would not always be that way.

"Start by doing what's necessary, then what's possible and suddenly you are doing the impossible."

Francis of Assisi

CHAPTER TWENTY-ONE

May 5, 1893
Eagle Valley

"Going for a ride on Sugar, Bear is going with me." Abby yelled to her mom as she went out the door. It was a nice spring evening, they had been to church that morning and had pot luck dinner with the family after church. When they finished eating they had bible study, Abby was ready for some fresh air.

She went to the barn and saddled Sugar, Bear waited at the door. Sugar was a young filly, a cross between a wild mustang and the son of the Tennessee Walking Stallion Blue Eagle that her grandfather brought from his home after the Civil War. She was as smooth to ride as a rocking chair and she loved to run.

May 12, 1865 Wilbur Plantation Tennessee

With remorse and dread beginning to knock at his heart, Wade Wilbur, a young Confederate lieutenant viewed the plantation he had known as a boy. Slowly he walked through the burned and charred rubble. What had once been a mansion of a home with ornamental white pillars out front had been reduced to ashes. Anger and emptiness spread through him. It was a time of agony and defeat for the South but somehow he never thought it would reach his home.

He remembered the cotton fields, the smell of tobacco curing and most of all the champion horses. Where were his parents? Where were the darkies that worked the fields, once rich, now burned black?

Wade heard a noise and his hand found the Army Colt at his side. Walking around a pile of rubble he saw an old Negro sorting through some of the charred remains of what had once been his father's study. The man was old beyond his years, beard and hair silvery, face weathered and worn. He looked weak, gaunt and lacking the strength to carry his body erect. Wade could not believe it was Jess, the slave who was more like an uncle than a servant.

Jess? Old Jess? It had to be him. Who else could it be? Jess had been born and raised and lived all this life on the Wilbur plantation. Yes, it was Jess.

Wade took a tentative step. His foot crunched down on a broken pane of glass, shattering it and the silence. The sound startled him more than Jess. Old Jess heard the noise created by Wade's ill-placed boot and craned is head in Wade direction. At the sight of the tattered gray uniform, a spark of recognition brightened his tired eyes.

"Master Wade?" He inquired in that inimitable drawl of southern Negroes. "Is that you, Master Wade?"

Wade increased his pace. "Yes Jess, it's me" his vision blurring with tears.

Jess met him at the crumbled foundation. They embraced, crying, consoling, reviewing and wishing for happier times.

"Where are my parents?" Wade asked, suspecting the answer.

"Gone. Both gone." Jess could hardly get the words out. "One hammering blow after another and your daddy's will to live be torn away. You was all he had left and he got word that you was lost in action, it was just too much. Your mama lasted only a few

days after Master Charles passed on. They is with the Lord now."
Old Jess fell silent.

Frustration, anger and emptiness. Wade had never felt anything
like it before. The lump in his throat made it impossible to talk.
He felt like a little boy having a bad dream. He had looked forward
so much to coming home and now to find this.

Wade was long-geared, raw boned, arms heavy with muscle.
His shoulders were wide but right now he was weak as a kitten.
The Civil War had been pure Hell for him but the horrors of
combat were a distant hollow memory compared to the emotional
pangs he felt at this moment.

Jess showed him the graves of his parents. He had put up fine
markers.

Charles Wilbur Martha Wilbur

1800-1865 1808-1865

"Dear Lord, I pray for You to guide me. I do not ask for
smooth paths or an easy load. Have me remember the lessons of
my mother and father. I pray thou will look on them tenderly as
they have endured so much."

Old Jess took the young man's arm and led him away. "Some
casks of wine and whiskey fell into the hands of them Yankee
soldiers. They got drunk. Burned and looted. I could see fires
everywhere." Confederates as well as the Union army tended to
live off the land they passed through taking what was needed. The
land and people suffered greatly.

"What about Eagle?" Wade asked hesitantly.

"A Yankee captain took a real shine to Blue Eagle. Yanks got
themselves a garrison where the Creswell Tobacco Company was."
Jess paused. "That there Yank wants to geld Eagle and make him
his parade horse."

"I have to get Blue Eagle," Wade said softly. He didn't know
how. He only knew if he didn't try it would always be like he

had let his father's dream die. Wade knew the Creswell Tobacco Company well, as a boy he had played there. He did not want to become a horse thief but he couldn't see any other way.

That young Confederate lieutenant was Abby's grandfather. She had heard many stories of the large Tennessee plantation where her grandfather grew up and of his trip to Colorado by wagon train.

Chet looked out the open door of his shop to see Abby and Bear leave the yard. It was hard for him to believe his baby girl was growing up and old enough to go for a ride by herself.

About a half hour later he noticed Bear coming toward the building site. Bear was not in his usual dog trot he was running like his tail was on fire. Chet hung up his leather apron and stepped out of the shop as Bear came into the yard. He spun to a stop and barked at Chet as he turned to go back the way he had come. Chet ran to the barn to saddle his horse and in minutes was following Bear.

Mounting a small rounded hill Chet saw what he feared. Sugar sprawled on the ground and laying ahead of her a good ten feet was Abby. Sugar was making an attempt to get to her feet but Abby lay still. Chet slid his horse to a stop and dismounted on the run. He got to Abby just as she was coming to. She had a scrap on her cheek, blood was making its way through grass stain and dirt. Both of her elbows were bleeding and she was gasping for air. Chet fell to the ground next to her and cradled her in his arms. She looked at him with glazed eyes that were full of pain.

Bear looked to the north and saw Wade checking the new foals. He ran toward him barking. Wade mounted on a tall black gelding could see Chet and Abby on the ground. He put his spurs to his mount and raced with Bear to them.

Chet was carrying Abby to his horse when Wade arrived. He dismounted and held Abby while Chet mounted his horse.

"She had the wind knocked out of her and was in great pain until she caught her breath. I don't know if she has any broken bones, will get her to Carmen. Will you see to Sugar?" Chet turned his horse and slowly headed toward their homestead.

"Sure. I will be there as soon as I can." Wade walked to where Sugar struggled to get to her feet. He saw her right front leg was broken. The bone just above the fetlock was sticking out of the skin. He saw the hole she had stepped in at a full run that caused the spill. Her weight and speed was more than the slender bone could support.

Chet heard the report of his father's colt revolver and knew he did what had to be done. Abby heard it too and for the first time tears came to her eyes. The tears running down through the blood and dirt on her face as she sobbed. Bear running ahead stopped for only a moment when he heard the gunshot. Reaching the cabin door he stood on his hind legs and pulled the latch string to open the door and barked for Carmen as he entered.

"What is it Bear, what has you so upset?" Coming to the open door Carmen saw Chet with Abby in his arms coming into the yard. She could hear Abby sobbing, her breath coming in short quick bursts. She assumed it was from pain and not from the grief of losing her friend. She ran off the porch to the hitch rail. She reached up and took her baby girl in her arms and carried her into their cabin.

Abby continued sobbing. The pain in her heart was greater than the pain from her wounds. Carmen was cleaning her wounds with warm water and a cloth, being as gentle as she could. So far she could not find any broken bones.

"Where do you feel the most pain Abby? Where does it hurt the most?"

"I killed my best friend, I will never ride again." The words came out in short quick gasps as she sobbed. "I should have seen that hole, I should not have been riding so fast." It was difficult for Carmen to understand her words as they were mixed with tears of sadness.

Chet was standing back wishing he could do something for his little girl. Something, anything to help take away her pain. He wished he had the magic words to comfort her. He just watched as Carmen doctored up the superficial wounds. Very soon Abby drifted off to sleep, exhausted, worn out from her ordeal.

Wade came in the cabin to find Chet and Carmen praying for Abby to have the strength and courage to overcome her sadness.

"It was not a fresh hole, there was no dirt or sign of activity around it. It was not like she recklessly rode into a Prairie Dog colony. There was no way Sugar or Abby could have seen the hole. I brought in the saddle and bridle. I will go get my stone boat* and bring Sugar in. Don't want to leave Sugar out there all night, I will take the boys to help me. I know it is not what we normally do, but I think it is best if we dig a grave and bury Sugar. I think this is what is best for Abby." Wade did not wait for a reply but turned and walked out of the cabin, leaving Chet and Carmen to ponder what he had said.

It was not an easy task to dig a grave for such a large animal. Chet and the boys worked with pick and shovel for several hours. In his effort to give a good answer to Carlos and Wy why it was necessary to dig the grave, Chet arrived at one for himself. In the midst of attempting to answer questions for others our minds often become uncluttered and clear.

Their work completed, they cleaned their tools and put them away. Their muscles were tired and aching as they made their way to the cabin. It was a good feeling in spite of their pain, they felt good about a tough task well done.

---

* A stone boat is a flat-bottomed sled used for transporting stones and other heavy objects.

The graveside service for Sugar gave Jobob the opportunity to impress on Abby and remind all the adults, that bad things happen to good people and animals. That many times it is out of our control how things turn out. When we have done our best we should accept the results without peril and not add to our punishment.

"It is sad to have a companion die under any circumstances, by any means. More so when the companion dies tragically or violently. It always leaves us somewhat bewildered. Lord, we ask that you take Sugar into your flock. Gracious Father, Ecclesiastes reminds us that for everything there is a season. Knowing this does not make the loss of a friend any easier. In this time of mourning, may those who are bereaved be grateful for the relationship and memory of this faithful companion. Amen."

Jobok knew that Abby was in no condition to hear his words and suddenly feel better. He hoped that later she could reflect on them and get over the guilt she now felt. This was the first burial for the people of the valley of a large animal. They could only imagine the pain Abby was feeling but they wanted to do as much as they could to help her through this ordeal.

"Guilt is always hungry, don't let it consume you."

Terri Guillemets

CHAPTER TWENTY-TWO

Chet and Carmen's Cabin
June 5, 1893

They were all at the breakfast table eating hot cakes with maple syrup and pork belly. Bear was by Carlos hoping he would drop a hunk of pork belly.

"These are awesome pancakes Mom." Carlos reached for the plate for his second helping. Chet chuckled loud enough for Carmen to hear.

"Don't you start something you can't finish Mr. Wilbur." Carmen handed Carlos the maple syrup as she spoke.

"What? What shouldn't dad start?" Abby wanted to know. Chet didn't say a word, he continued to eat but he had a grin from ear to ear. "Come on Mom, tell us. Is it something about pancakes?"

"You may as well tell your funny story now Wilbur." When Carmen called him Wilbur, Chet knew he was in trouble.

"I don't have anything to tell." Chet said it but his grin told a different story.

"Come on, now you have us all curious." Carlos spoke but Abby and Wy were also eager to hear the story.

"It's nothing it happened years ago when we were first married." Carmen got up to get the coffee pot.

"Speaking of that, we have an anniversary coming up." Chet made an attempt to change the subject. "In a few days we will be married fifteen years."

"No, don't change the subject dad, what about the pancake story?" Carlos had stopped eating and was waiting for one of them to tell what happened.

"If you must know, my mother taught me to cook and I was rather good with Mexican dishes. She never made pancakes and your father loves pancakes. So when we were first married I attempted to make some as a surprise. They were so bad that he could barely force them down. They were lumpy, doughy and the more he ate the more annoyed I become."

"So dad pretended that he liked them?" Abby asked.

"Yes and that made me angry because I knew how terrible they were."

"What this thing, anniversary?" Wy wanted to know.

"It's the day we were married."

"That is important to you?" Wy was still learning the ways of white people.

"Yes, but the fifteenth is not an important anniversary. It is crystal." Carmen was happy to be talking about something other than her first attempt to make pancakes.

"What this crystal?" Wy asked.

""Crystal is a fancy type of glass. They make bowls, candlesticks and other things out of it." Chet too was glad to escape the pancake story. He had got a pair of crystal candlestick holders from Dusty for Carmen, so he was all set for their anniversary.

There were dark rain clouds rolling in from the west when they got up from the breakfast table. "Better hurry and do chores, looks like we are going to get a much needed rain." Chet and the boys went outside and Abby helped her mother clear the table and do the dishes. Bear was busy with the left-overs from breakfast.

He liked pancakes but he loved pork belly. Later that morning it started to rain, a nice easy rain. No wind, no noise just a steady rain. It rained on and off all afternoon and into the evening and was still raining when Carlos woke up the next morning. He could hear his mom and dad moving around in the kitchen.

"Where's Wy?" He asked as he came down from the loft.

"We haven't seen him this morning, thought he was up there with you but we found this note on the table." Chet had a hot cup of coffee and was seated at the kitchen table, he handed Carlos the note to read.

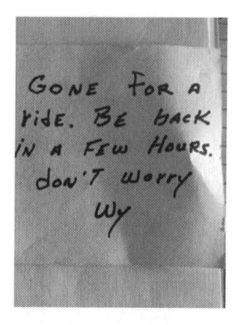

GONE for a
ride. BE back
in a Few Hours.
don'T worry
Wy

"Are we going to look for him?" Carlos laid the note on the table.

"The rain has washed out all his tracks and his scent, Bear wouldn't even know which way to start." At the mention of his name, Bear got off his deer skin and went to Chet.

"Are you mad at him?"

"We are more disappointed than we are angry." Carmen picked

up the note to read it for the umpteenth time. "We realize that Wy's background is so different from yours that we feel sure he thinks there is nothing wrong with what he has done."

Wy tied his horse at the hitch rail of the Bear Lake trading post. He took off his yellow oil slicker and shook the rain off of it. He folded it and laid it over his saddle. He took his .22 and entered the trading post.

"Wy, what brings you to Bear Lake?" Dusty was standing by the cash register.

"Want anniversary gift for Chet and Carmen."

"How much were looking to spend?"

"Want to trade my rifle for gift." He held up his rifle for Dusty to see.

"Didn't you get this for Christmas?" Dusty took the .22 and checked to make sure it wasn't loaded.

"Yes, it is the best thing that I have. You have crystal?"

"We don't have any crystal, had a pair of candlesticks but Chet got them for Carmen. Do Chet and Carmen know that you are here?" Dusty couldn't help but see the disappointment in Wy's face.

"I leave them note not to worry I would be back in few hours. I want to surprise them with gift." Sarah with her toddler on her hip came from their living quarters. She had heard just enough to get the drift of the situation.

"What do your people give each other on specials occasions, Wy?" Sarah asked as her boy reached out his arms to his father. Dusty took him and held him high over his head before putting him down to stand by him. He was glad to turn this situation over to Sarah.

"Blankets are associated with important events in my village."

"We have several authentic blankets that may interest you. Let me show you what we have." She moved down the middle aisle and took a star quilt off the shelf. She held it up so that Wy could see the design. "This is a nice heavy blanket. We also have this blanket that is labeled the way of life. It has a buffalo on it which is the symbol of unity, dignity, valor and strength. As you know the buffalo sustained all life for the Plains Tribes. This is a Pendleton Blanket."* She held it up for Wy to see.

"You trade me this for my rifle?" Dusty came down the aisle with his son holding on to his finger as they slowly walked up to where Wy and Sarah were.

"No. I can't take your rifle in trade. But we do need some beaver pelts. Sarah, could we let Wy take this blanket and pay us in beaver pelts later this fall?" Dusty wanted to help. He knew Wy would be in enough trouble as it was without coming home lacking his Christmas gift.

*Native Americans have acknowledged births, deaths, and major milestones and accomplishments with the gift of a Pendleton blanket.

"If we can't trust Wy, I don't know who we can trust. Is there anything else that you need Wy?" She put the star quilt back on the shelf and folded the Pendleton before handing it to Wy.

"No, just need gift for Carmen and Chet. Is this nice gift?" He ran his hand over the blanket as he asked.

"Yes, that is a very nice gift, I am sure they will be pleased with your gift. I do not think they will be pleased that you came without asking their permission." Wy's eyes showed he was in deep thought, the expression on his face told them he did not understand why Carmen and Chet would be displeased with him. He thought he was doing something nice for them.

"Would you like for me to wrap the blanket for you?"

"Yes, please and thank you for helping me. I will get you many nice beaver pelts this fall." He handed Sarah the blanket. She took it and wrapped it in brown paper and tied it with string.

"A couple of nice beaver pelts should cover this and leave you with enough for some shells and rock candy." She handed Wy his gift and could not help but notice how pleased he appeared.

> "Presents are made for the pleasure of who gives
> them, not the merits of who receives them."
>
> Carlos Ruiz Zafon

CHAPTER TWENTY-THREE

June 7, 1893
Chet & Carmen's Cabin

Wy opened his sleepy eyes and looked around in the dim light of the loft. Mr. Sun was hiding behind dark rain clouds. As he stretched all he could hear was the rain on the roof. He could see no light coming up from the kitchen or hear any noise. He looked and saw that Carlos's bunk was empty. Puzzled, he crawled out of his bunk and put on his clothes.

Going down the ladder to the kitchen not even Bear was there to greet him. It was empty, the whole house was empty. He wondered what was going on as he saw his note on the kitchen table. He picked up the note and looked at it in deep thought. It was if they had left it there for him. He looked at it again and read it out loud. "Gone for a ride. Be back in a few hours don't worry Wy"

He went to the window and looked out into the yard, there were small pools of water everywhere but no sign of anyone. He went to the coat rack and put on his slicker and hat and walked out to the barn. It was more of a mist than it was rain and he could see it was starting to clear up in the west.

He saw that the surrey and team were gone from the barn. He

got his horse, saddle him, mounted and rode to the school/church. He saw Kemp coming out of his barn.

"Good morning Wy. What brings you here in the rain?"

"Looking for Chet and the family, have you seen them this morning?"

"No. They leave without letting you know where they were going?"

"There was a note on the kitchen table."

"What did it say?"

"It said, 'Gone for a ride. Be back in a few hours don't worry Wy'." He didn't tell Kemp it was the same note that he gave them a couple days ago.

"Well, I wouldn't worry, they should be home soon, and they may even be there when you get back." Kemp could see Wy was upset. "You want to come in and have some breakfast?"

"No thanks, I will go back to the cabin." Wy turned his horse and rode slowly south toward their cabin.

Meanwhile, In Bear Lake Chet and the family were enjoying breakfast with Dusty and Sarah. "So you guys sneaked out leaving Wy sleeping?" Dusty had a big grin on his face.

"Yes, we needed a few supplies and we wanted to surprise Wy with a couple of those russets for his horses bridle." Chet took a sip of his hot coffee.

"I have a feeling there is a teaching moment in this someplace." Sarah said as she got up to get the coffee pot and refill their cups.

"We are hoping that is the case." Carmen said as she held out her cup to Sarah. "Wy is a fine young man and he is learning our language and our ways. English words have so many different meanings I am sure it is difficult for Wy at times to know what we mean. We talked it over and thought an example could be worth a thousand words."

"If nothing else, I am sure you got his attention." Dusty helped himself to another pancake. "I could tell when Wy was here that he did not feel he had done anything wrong."

"No. In fact he feels that he did something very good for Mom and Dad." Carlos took the last pancake and handed the empty plate to Sarah.

"Anyone want more pancakes, I can make some more?" There was a chorus of 'no thanks' and people shaking their heads.

"We do want you to hold Wy to his word. We want him to pay you with some beaver pelts this fall." Carmen finished her coffee and pushed back her chair to help Sarah clear the table.

"We will do that. Wy saw me write it down and put the paper up on the wall by the register so that I don't forget."

A few hours later Wy stopped pacing the floor when he heard the surrey come into the yard. He watched out the window as they unloaded the things they got at Bear Lake. Carlos took the team and surrey to the barn as the others came to the Cabin. Once inside they placed everything on the big kitchen table.

"Where have you been, I was worried?" Wy asked.

"Didn't you read the note? It said not to worry." Carmen started to put things away.

Wy looked at her as if he was starting to understand. "So this was my punishment?"

"Did you think you were punishing us when you did this very same thing?" Chet asked and could see Wy was beginning to understand.

"We were not punishing you Wy, we wanted to surprise you with these." Carmen handed him the fancy shining russets for his horses bridle.

Wy took the russets and looked into the eyes of Carmen and Chet. He did not see any anger or even disappointment. He saw happy, smiling eyes.

"No, I was not trying to punish you. I am sorry, I did not mean to be disrespectful. I now know what it is like to wake up and be worried, to wonder what is going on, where everyone is."

"We know you didn't mean any harm and that you were not being disrespectful. In fact we know that in your own way you were showing us respect. We just wanted you to feel what it was like and now you know." Carmen came around the table and gave Wy a hug. This action always made him feel good and uneasy at the same time.

The remainder of the afternoon and evening they spent having a chess tournament. They had two complete sets so they could have two matches going at the same time. The other player could move between the two matches learning moves and strategies. Carmen and Chet always were in the finals of the tournaments as they did not play to let their children win. They knew the time would come when their children would beat them but it was something their children would have to earn.

Chet however, would play very carefully once in a while to allow Carmen to win. He had to do it with skill and caution because if she ever felt he was playing to let her win, she would be very angry and Chet did not want Carmen to be upset with him. What Chet did not know was that Carmen would do the same thing. A few of their games ended in a draw. A king and one bishop versus a king cannot create a checkmate. For the most part a draw would occur for them when it appeared that neither of them could win quickly and it was bed time.

Carmen and Chet both felt that the game of chess helped the children learn life skills. Helped them to develop the ability to perform a mental task. With Wy playing it was ideal for teaching that although we may come from different backgrounds, speak different languages, our minds tend to work in a similar way when trying to reach a goal. They also learned that during the games the children were more apt to share their feelings and difficulties if something was on their mind. It was during a match with her dad that Abby had some questions.

"Dad when I play Carlos he chuckles as he makes his move and that annoys me."

"Yes I can understand how you feel, it is best just to ignore it. He is trying to annoy you so that you can't concentrate on the match."

"When I play Wy and move my castle he will move his and castle on the same side I do. What can or should I do?"

"Wy is not a riskless player. When he does that it is harder for you to make a direct attack on his king. Your king is also more protected so this move tends to slow down the game."

"So are you saying that how the boys play chess tells something about them? "What does it say about me?

"It says that you are observant and strive to do your best."

"I just strive for the ability to beat those two boys."

"The greatest ability is dependability."

Curt Bergwall

CHAPTER TWENTY-FOUR

Chet and Carmen's Cabin
June 15, 1993

"Kemp has been working with a young filly, wanted to make her a buggy horse for Pat. He told me that when he put the harness on Spice and hitched her she looked and acted like she had been beaten. Her head was down and she carried it to one side and her ears were flat but when he put the saddle on her she looked like a million bucks. Head was up proud and ears forward. Pat did not needing a saddle horse. He turned her out with the herd. On the way home I cut Spice out of the herd and put her in the box stall in the barn." Chet reached for the plate of venison steaks, they were enjoying their evening meal.

"There you go Abby, you can ride her up to the lake tomorrow." Carlos took the plate of steaks from his father and helped himself.

"No thanks." Abby didn't look up from her plate. "I have a book I want to finish so I won't be going up to the lake."

"Abby, I know how you love the lake." Carmen went to the stove to get more coffee for her and Chet. The lake was up on the rim of the canyon with only deer trails leading to it. There was no way a buggy or buckboard could get up there. It was a clear blue lake, spring fed and was too cold to swim in until the middle of

June. This would be their first trip of the summer to swim and fish for the lake trout.

"You should at least check out this filly." Carlos reached for another steak.

"Unless that is Sugar out there in the box stall I am not interested." Abby got up from the table and ran outside. Bear looked at her and at the venison he knew Carlos and Wy would be slipping him. He also knew where he was needed so he followed Abby.

"What are we going to do, the longer she waits the more difficult it is going to be?" Carmen filled their coffee cups and replaced the pot to the back of the stove.

"I know how much she loves that lake, I thought for sure this would be the right time and the right horse." Chet took a sip of his fresh hot coffee.

They allowed Bear to comfort Abby as they discussed how they could best help her. Wy came up with the idea to saddle the new horse and put it at the hitch rail with theirs. They would not say anything to Abby let her make the decision. They all felt the more they pushed her the more stubborn she would be.

"It won't be the end of the world if she doesn't go up to the lake but I do not think it would be good for us not to go." Carmen remembered how stubborn she herself could be at Abby's age and how her father would allow her time to work it out.

The next morning they were busy doing the chores and packing things for their trip to the lake, No one said anything to Abby about going or not going. All the horses were saddled and at the hitch rail in front of the cabin. When it was time to mount up they went out the door without saying goodbye to Abby. As they rode out of the yard, Abby looked out the window and saw Bear and Spice still at the hitch rail. Spice was pawing the ground with her right front hoof and Bear was barking at the house.

With her family out of sight she went outside and walked up to the young filly. Spice let out a soft, low whinny and reached out her head toward Abby. Abby was still a few feet away when Bear jumped up and with his front paws and gave her a push forward. It surprised her and threw her off balance, she grabbed the hitch rail to keep from falling. The quick movement startled Spice and she jumped back.

"Whoa girl, it's okay, I am sorry I scared you." She spoke in a soft voice. "Bear, see what you made me do?" She looked at Bear and he barked as if to say, "Well, get on the horse."

Spice came forward and with a soft neigh put her nose out toward Abby. Abby slid her hand up the side of Spice's head and smoothed out her foretop. She looked around to make sure she was alone. With no one watching she ducked under the hitch rail and unwrapped the reins. She put her left foot in the stirrup and swung up into the saddle. Spice didn't move as Abby just sat there feeling the power of a horse under her for the first time since her accident. To guard against and ensure that it wouldn't happen again she had avoided this. She could not pretend nothing had happened and tears came to her eyes as she remembered. It was hard to let go of the feelings she had that it was her fault.

Spice turned her head to look back and up at Abby. She was displaying perfect patience as she waited for Abby to give her a command. Abby wiped her arm across her eyes as she reached down with her other hand and patted Spice on the neck. "Sorry girl, must be hard for you to figure out why I am acting this way." Abby touched the reins to the side of Spice's neck and she turned away from the hitch rail and walked out of the yard. Bear watched and then jumped out in front to lead the way.

Some of the trail was steep and Abby had to lean forward and let Spice leap to make the climb. As Abby topped the rim of the canyon and looked down upon the lake she was glad that she had come. She had told her dad that someday she was going to build a house right here.

Photo by Mary Jo Hughes

She rode to where the other horses were grazing and noticed that her father's horse was not among them. She took hobbles out of the saddle bag and put them on Spice's front legs. She stripped off the bridle and saddle and put them with the others letting Spice go graze.

"Where's dad?" She asked as she walked up to where her mother had a blanket spread. The boys were already fishing. Bear went down to the lake to get a drink.

"He said he had something he needed to check on, that he would catch up." Carmen was making a circle of rocks so they could have a fire to fry the fish. There was a big black cast iron skillet full of butter waiting for the fire and fish.

"That something wouldn't be me would it?" Abby was sure she knew the answer to her question before she asked it.

"Your father didn't say but you are always on his mind and in his thoughts, even when it doesn't seem like it." Carmen had to smile at how this had worked out. She took comfort in the fact that they had allowed Abby to work it out and didn't force the issue. Abby seemed happy and relaxed after her first time on a horse since the accident.

"Mom are there horse doctors?" She was gazing off into the distance where the boys were fishing.

"Yes, I was reading about a school in Iowa in the Denver paper.* Why do you ask?"

"Well, if a man has a broken leg they fix it. Why can't they do that for a horse?"

"Because you can explain to a human that they have to stay in bed and hold the leg still. You can't do that with an animal. Do you think you would like to be an animal doctor, I think they are called veterinarians."

"I don't know, do you think I could?" She turned to look at her mother.

"Yes, you are a good student, you read well for your age and you have a good mind. We can see if we can find some books for you to read and learn more about it." Carmen was feeling so good about this new development.

"I know Gramps did the right thing for Sugar but I would like to find a way to do more. The other day dad and I found a dead cow down by the stream. I asked him why it died and he said he didn't know that it could have been one of several things. That got me to thinking about doing something to help animals when I grow up."

*As the nation's first public veterinary school, Iowa State

University's College of Veterinary Medicine takes pride in its heritage while shaping the future of veterinary professional practice, education, research and service.

"Wisdom is knowing what to do next, skill is knowing how to do it and virtue is doing it."

David Starr Jordan

CHAPTER TWENTY-FIVE

Union Station Denver, Colo.
July 4, 1893

Chet was standing in front of his team, waiting for the 1:00 PM train to arrive with the Texas visitors. The team was jumpy as people were celebrating all over Denver. That morning they had held a parade and in the distance Chet could hear a band playing John Philip Sousa's Washington Post March. *

People were shooting fire crackers and those without the money to buy them were shooting their guns in the air. Some were even throwing sticks of dynamite into the air to explode. They were celebrating the nation's 117th birthday and it was going to get very rowdy. Whiskey and gun powder do not mix well and they had an abundant supply of both.

Chet was glad that he had not allowed Bear to come with him. Bear had wanted to and followed the buckboard to the east gate of Eagle Valley before turning around and going back to the cabin. The noise was loud to Chet and made his ears ring it would have been ten times worse for Bear as his hearing is that much keener than Chet's. This was the reason Chet was having to stand at the head of his team and calm them. Horses can detect sounds man can't. They have a wider range of high-frequency tones, such as the squeak of a bat. In the horses natural environment (open plains) the horse had to hear the noise generated by predators. The snap, crackle and pop of grass or twigs under say a mountain lion's paws. The horse's natural instinct was to run away and that is what the team wanted to do.

Speaking softly to the team with a firm hold on their bridles was all that he could do as he waited. Fireworks have been a tradition of American's Fourth of July celebrations since the country's inception, with the founding fathers themselves using fireworks to mark the birth of our nation. It would only get worse with more and more joining in the celebration.

*In 1899, the owners of the Washington Post newspaper requested that John Philip Sousa, the leader of the United States Marine Band, compose a march for the newspaper's essay contest. Sousa obliged, "The Washington Post March" and it became popular.

The early fireworks were more for sound than show, it its simplest form gunpowder explodes quickly, making a terrific bang but not much to see. Over time people discovered that using chemical compounds with the gunpowder made the explosives burn brighter and longer. The multi-hued displays began in the 1830s, when Italians added trace amounts of metals that created colors.

Denver was in a depression. President Grove Cleveland oversaw the repeal of the Sherman Silver Purchase Act and the price of silver dropped from eighty-three cents to sixty-two cents an ounce. With almost everything in Colorado tied to mining in one way or another the depression hit the state hard. Unemployed miners flooded Denver in hopes of finding work. A tent city appeared in Riverfront Park along the South Platte River.

These men were angry. They were hungry and the 4th of July celebration gave them an excuse to blow off some steam. The jail in Denver would be over flowing by morning.

Later that night fireworks would be in the air over Cripple Creek, these along with the acts of careless men would keep the firemen busy. The cedar shingles on the roofs of homes and businesses catch on fire rather easy and the tents could not withstand a hot ember. Both the police force and the firemen would have a busy night.

Looking toward Union Station Chet saw his guests from Texas. He waved to them but could not go help carry their luggage as he could not take a chance and let go of the team.

"Sorry I couldn't come to help, this team of horses don't understand what the 4th of July is all about." Chet held the team with one hand and extended the other to Jake. "How was your trip?"

"Linda showed John and Susan how to play the "Cat's Cradle" string game. They got good at it and passed it back and forth, they can't wait to show Carlos and Abby the magic of the game." Jake climbed up on the spring seat.

"Even with the games and Lucky for company the train couldn't go fast enough for them to see your children and get to this valley they have heard so much about." Linda was with the children in the back.

"The kids wanted to come meet the train, they were very disappointed when they found out it wasn't in the cards." Chet waited until all were loaded and Jake had hold of the reins before he let go of the bridle. The team could not stand still, they pranced with excitement each time a fire cracker or gun shot went off.

Once up on the spring seat with Jake, Chet took the reins and let the team dance away from the hitch rail. They would love to run but Chet held them to a trot as they pulled away from the station. Once out of the station and away from any buildings the kids got their first look at the Rocky Mountains.

"Wow, look at that! Is that snow up there on the top?" John was pointing to a snow capped peak off to the west.

Photo by Mary Jo Hughes

"Yes, some of the high peaks have snow the year around." Jake remembered his first view of the Rockies. They were much different from the mountains in Tennessee that he remembered as a small boy. He was about John's age when he came to Colorado on the wagon train and first saw the Rockies.

They could still hear the celebration going on in Denver but it was fast fading in the distance as the team was making good time as they headed north. Chet wanted to be back in Eagle Valley before the fireworks filled the sky over Denver and more craziness hit the city.

"My early childhood memories center around the typical American country store and life in a small American town, including 4th of July celebrations marked by fireworks and patriotic music played from a pavilion bandstand."

Frederick Reines

CHAPTER TWENTY-SIX

Church/School Eagle Valley Evening, July 4, 1893

Abby was disappointed to the point of tears. She had dreamed of Lucky running to her and jumping into her arms. This was not the case, in fact Lucky did not want to get away from Susan. The ride from Texas on the big iron horse was scary but nothing like the sound of war in Denver when they got off the train. The bouncy ride in the buckboard to Eagle Valley with this cool mountain air and high altitude and now this huge mass of people. The little seven month old pup did not know what to think but he did not want to get away from the safety of his human.

"Let us pray. God did not send His son into this world to condemn the world but to save the world. We often sing that Jesus loves me, Jesus really does love us. Thank you Lord for giving us this simple faith that trusts Your promise to give us life forever in heaven. May this food we are about to partake strengthen and nourish our bodies so that we may do thy will. Amen." Jokob had a knack of saying in a few words what some preachers would take an hour to say. To a chorus of "Amen," Jokob took his customary place at the head of the line to fill his plate.

They were all gathered at the church/school for a big pot luck dinner. The whole valley was there and there was enough food for twice that many people. Sarah would play the organ and they would all join their voices in praise to their Lord. Bear was curled up in his spot by the door, he knew that once the plates were scraped he would have a feast. He guessed he could share it with this new pup that seemed to be making Abby unhappy.

Sharing was something that happened daily in Eagle Valley. Each family controlled their own holdings but they all helped each other with the tasks. They all used the Eagle brand on their cattle and horses but each of them had a little different mark so they could tell who owned the ones going to market. They sold cattle and horses to the army and the Indian agents. The price of silver had hurt Colorado but not Eagle Valley so much. Each family had a milk cow, some chickens and a small garden and even with the depression in Denver the army and the Indian agents still needed horses and cattle.

Bear had his duties, during the school year he would escort the kids to school and then make a round of the valley. He would get a treat from each of the housewives. It was a few days later when he was making this swing of the valley that he came upon a situation. His first stop was always at the west end of the big box canyon, at Jokob and Sarah's cabin. They were the oldest members of the valley, the parents of Kemp who married Pat the school teacher, James who married Denise and Judith who married Wade.

This morning as he neared the cabin he sensed something was wrong. The door was open and as he slowly entered he saw the back of a stranger. His clothes were rags and he was as dirty as his clothing. In his hand he held an old black powder cap and ball pistol that was pointed at Jokob and Sarah.

"You look to be down on your luck but that gun is not the answer to your problems, in fact it will only add to your problems." Jokob spoke softly but there was no sign of fear in his words.

Bear let out a deep, low, angry growl, a warning to the man

standing before him. At the sound of this the man swing around and pointed the gun at Bear.

"This your dog? Best call him off if you don't want him shot." The warning bounced off Bear like water off a ducks back. He curled back his lips and showed this stranger his fangs.

"Bear belongs to my great grandson and if you were to shoot him the whole valley would hunt you down and you would wish you had never been born." Jokob's words again were soft and matter of fact but they hit a nerve.

"I wish that all the time." The guttural sound coming from Bear's throat and Jokob's words put doubt in the young intruder's eyes.

"Why don't you just put the gun down and I will fix you something to eat, get you some of James old clothes. There is a wash basin just outside and a bucket of water." Sarah turned her back on him and slowly walked away. Just as slowly the young man laid down the gun.

"Ain't loaded anyway. I took a shot at a rabbit day before yesterday. Missed the rabbit and didn't have anything to reload with." Matt Glover continued to tell Jokob and Sarah his sad story. He had come out from Ohio and got a job in a silver mine, the pay was good but everything in camp was expensive so he lived from payday to payday. When the price of silver dropped the mine closed and he couldn't find work. He sold everything he had of value to get something to eat and a few days ago he just started walking. When he came to the rim of their box canyon and looked down he thought he was looking at paradise. He saw the cabin, the out buildings, the chickens, a milk cow, horses and cattle grazing up the valley. He found a deer trail and worked his way down the rock wall of the canyon to the valley floor.

Sarah placed a plate of food in front of him. Four eggs, a pile of pork belly and a large slice of bread with her blackberry jam on it. She got him a pair of James old bib overalls, a work shirt, some underwear and socks. She even had an old pair of boots that were a huge improvement over what he had on. They could be a little big but that was better than being too small.

Bear could see there was no longer a threat to Jokob or Sarah so when Sarah gave him a hunk of pork belly he turned and started toward Kemp and Pat's cabin which was next on his route. He would also make a stop at Sweeny and Penny's cabin as well as Wade and Judith's before going home to Chet and Carmen's cabin.

"You can find a place in the barn to sleep and I will give you enough odd jobs to pay for your keep. The next time we go to Denver you can ride along." Jokob had made the decision that the young man was not a danger to them. He had been fooled in the past but this time he felt good about his decision and he could see that Sarah agreed with him. Matt Glover was busy devouring the plate food Sarah had given him. He stopped just long enough to thank them for their kindness.

"Do all the good you can and make as
little fuss about it as possible."

Charles Dickens

CHAPTER TWENTY-SEVEN

Eagle Valley
July 8, 1893

Bear looked toward the cabin and saw Abby and Susan playing with the pup they called Lucky. He turned to see Carlos, Wy and John mounted and about to ride out of the yard. He thought it best that he follow the boys as they were more apt to need him. He moved at his steady trot, the boys going faster did not worry him as he knew he could always find them.

The boys rode to Sweeny's barn, dismounted and lead their horses inside. In a moment Sweeny came from his cabin to see what they were up to.

"Good morning boys, what brings you to my place?"

"We want to show John the secret canyon." Carlos pointed to the door in the back wall of the barn.

"Your grandfather and I have some young heifers in there with one of the Hereford bulls. We don't want them to be disturbed, we want them to get bred you best leave your horses here and go in on foot." Sweeny pointed to some box stalls that were empty that they could use.

The boys stripped off their saddles and put them on saddle pegs on the barn wall. They put their horses in the box stalls and took off their bridles and hung them on the horns of their saddles.

They got a pail of water and gave each of the horses a drink but none of the three were thirsty. Carlos's horse took just a sip and turned away to eat some hay in the manger. Wy's horse put his nose in the water and blew air splashing water on him. John's horse just walked away. They had not ridden that far and the horses had food and water before they were saddled.

"Chet and Jake know you boys are here?" Sweeny was watching and remembering how Chet and Dusty loved to play in the canyon pretending they were everything from wild Indians to lawmen after outlaws.

"Yes. Dad was telling us last night about Dull Knife and how you helped him and his small band." John wanted to see the actual existence of the door to the canyon.

"Dad said to be sure we told you we were going in." Carlos like the other boys was holding his .22 rifle.

"Don't be shooting around those heifers and you boys be careful and remember the safety rules." Bear came through the barn door just in time to go through the back door into the canyon with the boys.

The canyon floor was a carpet of lush grass, the sides were sheer rock walls. A spring coming out of the northeast corner formed a small pond that fed a stream running down the length of the canyon. The boys saw the herd of heifers and the Hereford bull grazing toward the far end of the canyon.

"Let's get a drink of this spring water, it is the best you will ever taste John." Carlos started toward the spring coming out of the canyon wall. Bear beat them to the water as he was lapping it up from the pond when they got there.

"So this is where Dull Knife hid from the U.S. Calvary?" John cupped his hands to get a drink from the spring.

The boys all had the power to form pictures in their minds. Looking out onto the valley floor they could plainly see Dull

Knife and his band, They could see the women putting thin strips of meat on racks to be dried in the sun. The men were decorating their ponies with paint and cloth tied to manes and tails. They could see Dull Knife sending three of his young braves to go and find the hunting party led by Hump Bull his first son. This hunting party had been gone from camp when the Calvary attacked and had no way of knowing where they were. Dull Knife wanted the hunting party to join them so they would be strong enough to defend themselves.

"We best put our rifles here by the spring, the braves did not have rifles." Carlos leaned his .22 up against the rock wall, Wy and John did likewise. The three started toward the far end of the canyon to find the narrow, steep and difficult ascend to the rim of the canyon. Jake had told them it was hidden by a large pine tree. They were on a secret mission for Dull Knife. The safety of the group depended on them finding a way out of the canyon and getting to Wyoming to find the hunting party. If they had to go out the way they came in the Calvary would find them for sure and send them to a reservation.

If they could find a way out of this canyon they could work their way north to the Rose Bud River where they knew there was good hunting and fishing. The winter would be very difficult and for that reason there were few white men and no soldiers in the area.

The three braves made their way to the west wall of the canyon. Their imagination was working overtime.

Photo by Mary Jo Hughes

They looked up at the sheer rock wall. It looked to be a hundred feet to the rim of the canyon. They worked their way north toward the stream that ran the length of the canyon and disappeared into the ground near the west wall.

In the north corner they found a large pine tree. The ground was covered with dead needles and the first branches of the tree were three feet or more off the ground. On their hands and knees they crawled under the big pine to the back wall. Bear followed them with ease. They found the old narrow deer trail that Dull Knife had used to leave the canyon and avoid the Calvary. The trail slanted toward the south and in several places water had washed part of it away and small pines had grown out of the canyon wall.

As the three would be Indian braves worked their way up the steep deer trail another group was working their way toward the rim of the canyon.

Mountain lion kittens learn hunting skills through play and

by watching their mother. At about six weeks of age the mother begins taking her kittens to her kill to feed. The kittens are covered with black-brown spots and have black tipped ears and a dark ring around their tail. One of North America's biggest cats an adult female can weigh over a hundred pounds and she will vigorously defend her kittens. This female had made a kill and had hid the carcass of a fawn near the top of the trail the boys were climbing. The cougar a powerful predator, tawny to light cinnamon in color, was followed by her three kittens as she made her way to her kill.

There was a slight breeze coming over the rim from the west and Bear picked up the scent of the big cat. The boys were beginning to pant from their steep climb up the face of the rock wall and were surprised when Bear pushed his way past them and with the hair on his back standing up he began to growl. What surprised them even more was the sight of the mother puma that appeared just ten to twelve feet above them with her mouth wide open and fangs showing. Bear was as big as the puma but not near as quick and his fangs were not as long. His big paws were no match for her sharp claws. Yet he held his ground to protect his humans. The three boys turned in unison, their hearts in their chests were pounding like sledge hammers. The three Indian braves looking for a path to the rim, on a difficult mission for Dull Knife were all at once looking for a way to the valley floor and safety.

Bear did not want any part of this big cat if it could be avoided. The mother did not want to leap into a fight and leave her kittens but she would protect them with her life. Slowly Bear backed down the steep trail, he did not want to turn his back on this deadly predator. As the distance between them increased they both became less intense. The cougar had been as surprised as the boys, the breeze was at her back and she could not smell or see the boys and Bear until she heard Bear and looked over the rim.

The boys slipped and slid down the narrow and steep trail

much of it on their butts. They hurried as fast as they could hugging the rock wall so that they did not fall.

At the bottom of the trail behind the big pine tree the boys leaned up against the rock wall. Their faces wet with sweat and their hearts were still pounding in their chests as Bear joined them. Carlos bent down and gave Bear a big hug. "You saved our bacon Bear, I am so glad that you were there." Bear reached up and licked Carlos face as if he understood what he said.

"Yes, if Bear had not pushed past us, we would have walked right into that mountain lion."* John dropped to his hands and knees and crawled under the pine tree. He went straight to the stream to wash his face and have a deep drink of the cold string water. The other two boys and Bear followed his lead.

Their mission for Dull Knife was forgotten. The vison of the mountain lion was etched in their brains. Their surprise to see the big cat right on top of them with her mouth wide open, fangs glistening in the sun light, ready to leap was something they would remember forever. Even Wy who as a small boy had been taught not to show fear was failing to do so.

*Mountain lion, puma, cougar, panther—this cat is known by more names than just about any other mammal. But no matter what name you call it, it's still the same big carnivore.

"I thought that if we did not fall to our death we would be eaten alive. I can still see her teeth right in my face." Wy held out his hand at arm's length to show how intimate he felt the puma was to them. Bear came to him and leaned up against him. He put his arm around the big dog thanking him for his bravery.

Later that evening they asked Chet if he felt Bear could win a fight with the big cat. "No. He would fight to his death but the mountain lion has too many weapons. Her claws could rip his flesh and if she ever got her teeth into his throat or the nape of his neck it would be over."

"An adult cougar can bring down a bull moose or elk. They are so quick and powerful." Jake told them a story of how he and Sweeny had seen a mountain lion attack a bull elk. The bull outweighed the cat by more than four hundred pounds but the puma won the battle. Pound-for-pound, the cougar may be the fiercest carnivore stalking pry in Colorado.

"Dad, do you think Bear knew he was over matched?" John reached down to pat Bear who was laying at his feet.

"Yes, I think his instincts told him the big cat was too quick and powerful but I think his love for you boys was greater than his fear of the cougar. That is why he pushed past you boys and got between you and the big cat. I have seen this with horses. A horse's natural instinct when it smells danger is to run. I have seen a mare all by herself smell or see danger and she will turn tail and run. That same mare with a young foal at her side that cannot run real fast will stand her ground and fight."

"Being terrified but going ahead and doing what must be done—that's courage. The one who feels no fear is a fool and the one who lets fear rule him is a coward."

Piers Anthony

CHAPTER TWENTY-EIGHT

Eagle Valley
January 1894

It was the Lewis and Clark expedition of 1804 that set into motion many unforeseen events – beginning with the buffalo. This rich valley was the summer home to majestic herds of buffalo. When the leaves turned color and the nights grew colder the herds drifted south where they would spend the winter. The Native Americans would go with them as the buffalo were their most crucial means of survival. The buffalo signaled good health, happiness and prosperity to the Indian tribes. They were also a symbol of unity, valor and strength. The buffalo supplied them with all their needs from game dice to headdresses. The Native Americans wasted none of these big providers. This was not true of the buffalo hunters, they killed them only for their hides and left their carcass to rot on the prairie.

Now just ninety years later the herds of buffalo were replaced with Hereford cattle and horses wearing the Eagle brand. The valley was the home to five families that came west on one of the many wagon trains after the Civil War.

Bear knew nothing of this. He knew nothing of the hardships of these men and women that he so willingly answered to. He jogged past their new cemetery, located behind the school/church.

Bear had no idea what a graveyard was or that it was a special burial ground for loved ones. He did not know he would be the first laid to rest with a head stone from the rock wall of the canyon. Slowly but surely all the members of the valley would join him in the cemetery.

These days he could go nowhere without his sidekick who tended to stumble and fall for no reason. Through rough times and smooth, joys and trials, there is no greater gift on earth than family. Lucky was part of his family now and like so many members of families at times he could be a pain. Families can be fragile. They would cry and laugh together and sometimes hurt one another. Bear didn't always understand what was going on but he liked it when they were happy. He found no pleasure if there was quarreling and division.

Bear was right where he was supposed to be. Doing what he was supposed to do. Bear had a great commitment to his family. Everything that he did was with them in mind. He was thankful for this opportunity to serve. He did so many things that went unnoticed.

For example, he knew Abby did not like the darkness of night. If she had to go to the outhouse after dark he would escort her. She didn't have to call him or make a big deal of it, he just knew and was always there for her. The Colorado nights could be full of both beauty and scary shadows.

Photo by Rachel Rosenboom

Bear also knew that Carlos did not like liver, so whenever they would butcher and have fresh liver for their meal, he would sit next to Carlos. Carlos would slip him his liver. Just the smell of his mother frying it was enough to make Carlos feel sick to his stomach. Carlos would eat a small bite from time to time but he did not fool either Chet or Carmen. They both realized that it would not be the end of the world if he didn't eat the liver. They felt they did not have to act on everything they saw or heard.

Wy did not like cooked greens. They were soft and wimpy, he did not like the texture say nothing of the taste. These were also not one of Bear's favorite things to eat either. He would help Wy out just as he did Carlos but not with as much enthusiasm as liver was one of his favorite things to eat.

Carmen was full of spunk but she did not like mice. In the fall when the field mice were looking for a place to winter they would often get into the cabin. As bad as the mice were she hated it even more when Chet and Carlos would tease her. Bear would take care of them for Carmen.

Wherever he was needed, he was there. His presence always

giving comfort. If one of the family seemed to be sinking into sadness or suffering, Bear seemed to know. He was very good at reading body language. He could tell when one of the family was feeling depressed and needed a little Bear love. Just going to them and leaning against them was often enough to make them feel better.

However, as time passed, Bear turned over more and more of his duties to Lucky. He would still follow the children to school each morning but instead of doing his full round of the valley and going back to the cabin he would find a warm comfortable place in Kemp's barn to wait for them to be dismissed. One afternoon he wasn't there when the students came out, only Lucky was there to greet them. Carlos found Bear in the barn.

Showing the great respect the men of the valley had for Bear they built a fire in the cemetery to thaw the frozen ground so they could dig him a grave.

Photo by Rachel Rosenboom
The whole valley was there to say good-bye as Bear was truly

the valley dog. Lucky was more subdued than usual. Wy and Carlos placed Bear, wrapped in his deer skin, gently in the grave. Wy placed two Eagle feathers on the deer skin. Eagle feathers are an important symbol of the Native Americans way of life. They are a sign of respect and honor. Even Jokob had a tremble in his voice as he asked our Lord to take Bear into His flock.

In his short life, Bear demonstrated bravery, loyalty and most of all love. Perhaps like so many humans, Bear did not realize all the good that he had done and all the lives that he touched. . Bear was right where he was supposed to be, doing what he was supposed to do.

"The quality of a person's life is in direct proportion to their commitment to excellence, regardless of their chosen field of endeavor."

Vince Lombardi

POSTFACE

This is where the fiction ends and reality takes over.

Where are you supposed to be?

The answer to this question will vary greatly from individual to individual. It will depend on age and situation. Vocation includes everything that we are, not just employment. At the end of each day, everyone would like to give a thumbs-up to the question "What did I accomplish today?"

Why do some people succeed in life and others do not? Almost everyone needs affirmation from time to time as we all falter and fail. Is there anything that can help us to succeed in life?

Research tells us that there is no correlation between GPA and future success, no correlation between class rank and future success, no correlation between high test scores on ACT or SAT and future success. There is only one thing that shows a high correlation, that is success in extra-curricular activities. Success in band, vocal music, drama, FFA, Science Club, and or sports show a positive correlation. Of course you add in a high GPA, class rate and high test scores and the correlation is even higher.

To be in extra-curricular activities a student must pass up the after school coke dates. They must sacrifice, give of their time and energy for the good of the group. Maybe that is why there is such a high correlation, why only the bravest, most devoted will continue to come out year after year and work to make the team, the band,

and/or the group. Parents, fans and spectators can be a great help. They can help to produce the atmosphere and enthusiasm that make the game, the concert, the play or the group special.

This could be the reason there is a correlation. These students see that what they are doing is important to their parents and their community. This could be what is lacking in our big inter-city schools. The school does not give a high enough percentage of students a chance to succeed. These inter-city schools are not the main social hub of their community. Too many parents do not even know their students teachers or coaches.

Add to this good experience in school a good experience in church. These students see that it is important to their parents and the community for them to learn of God's word and know about good and evil. This shows them they are not left alone to battle sin and Satan. They have the power of their Lord and Savior to help them through the rough times in their lives. No, not everyone that is involved in extra-curricular activities will be a success in life and not everyone not in extra-curricular activities will be a failure in life, it is not that simple.

If a student lives in a household and hears nothing but negative comments about their school, about law enforcement, about their opportunities. If they witness parents and community leaders living a godless philosophy of doing whatever feels good at the time, hurting whomever they have to hurt to get their way, is it any wonder they have less chance of success? Is it any wonder that they drift toward street gangs?

Numerous studies have shown that owning a dog benefits a person's physical and mental well-being. Bear was right where he was supposed to be, doing what God put him on earth to do. His life was short compared to the humans but he made the most of each and every day.

Where are you supposed to be? As a high school principal in

Pomeroy, Iowa, Ken Wilbur asked that question several times each day for twenty years. A few times in those twenty years a student would look him straight in the eye and say; "I am right where I am supposed to be Mr. Wilbur, thanks for asking."

Does prayer help us to be where we are supposed to be?

We must remember when we pray for a victory that the people on the other side are also praying for a victory. When we pray for nice weather for our cookout, others are praying for it to rain for their garden or lawn. When we pray that a storm will miss us others could be praying for just enough wind and hail for some damage to roofs and cars so they can have work and are able to meet their payroll.

It was a Thursday in the late 1960's in a small Iowa school and the practice before a Friday night football game was short. They would run the plays they planned to use, go through the pre-game routine and stress defensive assignments. The players, mostly farm boys, would jump in their cars and head for home and something to eat. One senior boy driving a Buick Lark, either ran a stop sign or pulled out in front of a big station wagon flying over the hill. He was t-boned and they had to life-flight him to Des Moines.

Later that night the coach received a call from a sobbing mother, telling him that they had not even cleaned him up or dressed the wounds on his face. A team of doctors had examined him and said he would not last through the night. The coach went to bed with a very heavy heart.

The next morning at school they learned that the boy was still hanging on but not expected to live. The captain of the football team, who was also the President of the Student Body, came to see his coach. He said the seniors had talked and they did not want a pep meeting. They talked and decided that at the regular time for the pep meeting the students would all go to the gym and he would ask them, in their own way, to take a moment of silence for their teammate, classmate and friend.

On a normal Friday there would be horns honking, students yelling at each other and the cars leaving the parking lot would often spin a tire. Not this Friday, the cars pulled out slow, not even a radio could be heard.

That night after the game, the coach received a call from a crying mother. He was sure that they had lost this fine young man. Through her tears she told him that at around four that afternoon her son came out of his coma and told the nurse he was hungry. She said none of the doctors could believe it, they scurried around, cleaned him up and dressed his wounds. He was sleeping now and his mother was crying tears of joy and thanksgiving.

He faced a long and difficult road to recovery. But after years of rehab he went to college-graduated, got married and became a teacher and coach.

Do these parents, coaches and students believe in the power of prayer? Yes! Do they believe our Lord will answer all our prayers as we wish? No! The Lord does not answer all our prayers as we wish or as quickly as we wish.

There are many earthly situations where we do not know God's will but this we should know, that we should not fear the future but embrace it.

We could all make an attempt to pray for strength, courage and wisdom to handle the trials of each day. We could pray for strength, courage and the wisdom to make the correct decisions. We will never understand why some things happen. Maybe the loss of employment was to humble us and bring us closer to God. Maybe a health scare was to remind us of our mortality. Maybe the flat tire that made us late for work or school prevented an accident further down the road. We will never know but we can

have confidence knowing that our Lord is in charge if we allow
Him to be.

> "Success is walking from failure to failure
> with no loss of enthusiasm."

Winston Churchill

The Eagle Series of Novels:

Blue Eagle: The story of a young Confederate soldier at the end of the Civil War and his black stallion, Blue Eagle,

Eagle Valley: The story of how Native Americans and White settlers could line together in peace to the point of helping each other to survive.

Eagle Brand: Three Colorado men go to Texas and find more than they bargained for.

Eagle flight: A young baseball player from a little Iowa town goes to Chicago to play baseball for the Chicago White Stocking is entwined with the story of a young nun leaving the order to find out who murdered her father.

Luta: A young man who is half Native American leaves the safety of Eagle Valley and goes to the Hole in the Wall.

Bear: This is the latest in this series.

Another western romance novel:

Bona: A young Civil War veteran reluctantly teams up with a Catholic nun to right a wrong in the old West.

These fiction novels may be purchased on line at Authorhouse. com, Amazon, or Barnes and Nobel. You may also order them by calling 888-519-5121

About the Author:

Ken Wilbur spent thirty-four years working in the field of education in Iowa as teacher, coach and high school principal. In 1997 Ken moved to Abilene, Texas and purchased a dog kennel. Ken and his son Brent, raise, train and board some of the best bird dogs in Texas at Southern Hills Kennel.

Photo by Brent Wilbur

Your author was not a good student. He failed second grade and his report card was full of D's and F's in grade school. He was the last student to be picked for a spelling bee but one of the first for a sports game. His grades improved a little in Jr. high and in high school he had to maintain a C average to play sports. In college he did better but was still just an average student. After teaching for six years, his grades in grad school were much better. He graduated with honors and was invited to join the Phi Delta Kappa. He credits much of this positive change to the prayers of his mother. She always worried about him and prayed for him daily. (He was her favorite)

Your author hopes in some small way this will help others. His first novel was not published until after he had a bout with cancer and was almost eighty years old.